THE HAMLET

NP Novellas

Set 2:

Rowany de Vere and a Fair Degree of Frost – **Chaz Brenchley**
The Hamlet – **Joanna Corrance**
The Creator – **Aliya Whiteley**

Set 1:

Universal Language – **Tim Major**
Worldshifter – **Paul Di Filippo**
May Day – **Emma Coleman**
Requiem for an Astronaut – **Daniel Bennett**
Rose Knot – **Kari Sperring**
On Arcturus VII – **Eric Brown**
Fish! – **Ida Keogh**
My Mother Murdered the Moon – **Stephen Deas**
Visions of Ruin – **Mark West**
Entropy of Loss – **Stewart Hotston**
Telling the Bees – **Emma K. Leadley**
The Blackhart Blades – **David Gullen**

THE HAMLET
Joanna Corrance

NewCon Press
England

First published in the UK May 2025 by
NewCon Press
41 Wheatsheaf Road,
Alconbury Weston,
Cambs, PE28 4LF

NPN28 (limited edition hardback)
NPN29 (paperback)

10 9 8 7 6 5 4 3 2 1

ISBN:

978-1-914953-99-6 (hardback)
978-1-917735-00-1 (paperback)

Cover layout and design by Ian Whates
Utilising an image by Artspark

Editorial meddling and typesetting by Ian Whates

ONE
STAY INSIDE

It was an unusually hot day in early spring when all the screens turned black and the radios went silent. After a few moments, an announcement was made. A warning.

The message was simple: everyone was to return to their homes immediately and stay inside. Nobody knew what was happening as they retreated behind doors and barricaded their windows, but their unease was contagious.

In a small rural community in Scotland, the message didn't spread so quickly. Many of the residents remained outside enjoying their drinks and picnics while they basked beneath the warmth of the unusually pleasant afternoon sun, waving to their neighbours with broad smiles. As the news began to ripple amongst them, they glanced nervously at one another. Some of them laughed and dismissed any concerns, stating that they planned to remain outside to enjoy the glorious weather.

However, as their nervousness turned to an uncomfortable static in the air and the glaring heat became clawing, one by one, they crept inside until the clearing was empty. Before they shut their doors, they looked back out, maintaining their fixed smiles for the neighbours to see. Then, once the doors were shut and locked, they sat quietly with sombre expressions and wondered what was coming, unaware that as the days and weeks went by, the unusual events that were set to occur would creep into their little community and their stories would intertwine in the strangest of ways.

TWO

DOWN THE DRAIN

Beth

People talked about it as *'strange'*. They said things like *'when things got strange'* or they talked about their lives *'before things got strange'*. Nobody ever said *'creepy'*, or *'scary'*, or *'dangerous'* because that would be admitting that something really bad was happening. The word *'strange'* could mean something benign that we just didn't fully understand yet. Strange could be ok.

It pissed me off a bit that *'strange'* was the word they often used to describe me, as if I had something in common, or something to do with what was going on. Although, I noticed that they stopped calling me that pretty quickly after it all started, since by that point I practically blended in.

That was the problem with living in a tight-knit community, straddling the boundary between being rural and suburban, everyone knew you and everyone wanted to know your business. You were branded from day one.

My neighbour Helen McIvor had the most influence when it came to reputation within the community. The McIvor's lived in one of the bigger houses opposite mine. They were the kind of folk that I instinctively called 'Mr and Mrs McIvor' behind their backs and then struggled to recall their first names when I actually spoke to them. Mrs McIvor was one of those women who was involved in everything, whether it be the church, parent teacher association or allegedly harmless bitching. I imagined that she really struggled with things when they got *'strange'*. She was the kind of woman who could cook and bake all day and then step out on to her front porch without so much as a speck of flour on the front of her dress. People always thought she was charming when they first met her. I was never convinced.

Next door to me were Lisa and her daughter Polly. Since moving in, they had kept their distance which was fine by me. On the few occasions I had seen Lisa outside, she was drunk and looking furtively from side to side with bloodshot eyes, wary of people noticing. Mrs McIvor had always speculated on how she could afford to live in such a nice area, but as far as I was concerned it was none of my business. Lisa carried a haunted look about her which made me feel immensely sad. A couple of days prior, I had noticed little Polly wandering about outside my window wearing a strange costume. She waved at me and I waved uncertainly back, although I didn't go to check on her because I was frightened of Lisa seeing and thinking that I was criticising her parenting. Just because I felt sorry for her did not mean I wasn't scared of her.

The older residents in the community, the ones Mrs McIvor (quite rudely in my opinion) called 'the spinsters', had formed a tight-knit group. They rolled their eyes when they heard anyone refer to our community as 'the hamlet'; they called it a 'clachan'. I looked online and they were actually correct, but apparently newcomers had referred to it as 'the hamlet' until it stuck. The elderly ladies were usually found sat in a circle in one of their gardens, knitting over an open bottle of wine. They sold their work at the local arts and crafts fair in the nearby town and then spent their earnings on extortionate alpaca wool to repeat the whole process again. Since things turned strange, they had stayed very much hidden away, probably all sat in a circle inside one of their houses. I imagined it must be nice having friendships like that. Nobody knew too much about them, not even Mrs McIvor, but they didn't offend anyone or get involved in neighbourhood drama, so they had never been considered particularly gossip worthy.

Gossip often revolved around 'Matthew the pest' who rented one of the smaller bungalows at the other end of the hamlet. I would like to state for the record that I didn't give him that name; he was already branded with it by the time I moved in. He once told me my hair looked lovely, which I found quite sweet, until I realised that he was making fun of me. Then one day I overheard him shout over his fence at Jeanie that she had a *'cracking set'* as she was jogging by. Poor Jeanie didn't look like the kind of woman who would be accustomed to lewd remarks or gestures.

Jeanie lived in the beautifully renovated farmhouse up on the hill with her husband. The two of them looked expensive, an impossible thing to describe, but their beautifully pressed clothes and general glossiness exuded wealth. They had only moved in last year and everyone had been immensely curious about them. She had this way about her where she would breeze by with ease, like her feet barely touched the ground, and when she spoke her voice trickled on the verge of a song. We were entranced. Unfortunately, she kept to herself most of the time and hadn't left her house in a while. I hadn't seen her since I witnessed Matthew being rude to her.

I had inherited my house from my mum after she died. She always worried about me while she was alive, so it came as no surprise that she held onto the house so that she could pass it to me. That made me sad, since I'd have far preferred for her to have sold up and died in a deckchair on a hot beach somewhere, with a pina colada in one hand and a cigarette in the other. It's how she would have wanted to go.

The house had remained the same even with me living in it, all dated carpets and threadbare furniture. Everything was so old that it seemed to have faded into one neutral tone. The walls had once been magnolia, but Mum smoked so much that they were all discoloured and patchy where pictures had been moved about. When Mrs McIvor first came over with a hamper of goodies to welcome me to the hamlet and offer her condolences, she had looked around and winced, before suggesting all sorts of interior design ideas; mostly white gloss, skylights and pastel shades – just like her house. I mumbled uncomfortably and said I didn't want to change anything; I didn't have the energy.

11

As it turned out, I didn't have the energy for very much at all, particularly after Mum died. Cooking, cleaning, exercise, even personal hygiene. It just all seemed too much. The more the neighbours gossiped, the more I started hiding away, feeling a sinking sense of dread every time I stepped outside my front door. I knew that they were looking at the overgrown lawn, the broken tiles and the woman who had gained weight and stopped combing her hair. By the time things got strange, I'd already been ordering my shopping online for some time, so it didn't make too much of a difference for me, other than the fact I needed to book my delivery slot further in advance.

Unfortunately, confining myself like that had led to a build-up of mess. No, mess would be too kind. *Filth.* I'd like to have blamed the fact that the council didn't collect the bins any more, but in all honesty, the place had been getting bad long before things got strange. There were old pizza boxes, plastic film and cartons littering the floor, blocking some of the doors. As the temperature rose and the sun glared through the window, it had a greenhouse effect which made the smell drift unpleasantly. The kitchen was so bad that I had stopped using it altogether and ordered my food from one of the few takeaways that was still open in the town. The delivery driver knew to drop it off on the bathroom windowsill because that was where I spent my days. The bathroom was the nicest room in the house and the only room I had the energy to keep clean. All it took was a slide of a bleach-soaked cloth over porcelain and lino. It wasn't as difficult as cleaning the disgusting bedsheets and sticky fabric carpets that absorbed filth readily. Mums washing machine had long since broken, and even if I wanted to fix it, there was nobody I could call any more.

Each day I would run the bath so hot that my skin turned an angry pink and the rose smelling bubbles would disguise the pale rolls that had developed around my middle. The heat of the bath would give me a rosy glow that reflected pleasantly in the mirror as though I was wearing blusher. I would hold my breath for as long as possible and submerge myself, enjoying the dull silence of the water.

One day a pipe burst behind the wall. Overnight, the white wall behind the bath had turned an unpleasant paper mâché consistency and a steady stream began to form a pool over the floor, leaking out from beneath the skirting boards. I burst into tears when I found it the following morning, unsure of what to do.

"No, no, *no!*" I pushed my finger through the damp plaster as hot tears rolled down my cheeks. Not my lovely bathroom. Then I remembered: Matthew the pest was a plumber! I didn't have his number to hand, but I imagined someone must have it. I was certain he would have handed it out readily to female residents.

I began calling around.

'Beth, you really shouldn't be calling. Something weird is going on, I don't think we should be talking.'

'What the hell, Beth, why on earth would you even consider letting someone in your house with what's been happening? Just take a shower.'

'Ew, no. Why would I have Matthew's number?'

'Didn't you hear? Matthew was last seen wandering into the forest a couple of days ago. He hasn't been seen since. The police aren't even answering the phones any more so there's no point in reporting it.'

Growling in frustration, I threw my phone to the floor before pausing to consider if I might be able to source the problem; if anything, it could be a project for me. Digging my fingers into the mushy plaster, the wall came away easily and revealed a dark, cavernous space filled with heavy metal pipes that glistened from the damp and splayed out like the tangled legs of a spider. I clambered between them. *Strange.* The leak was at the very back where one of the pipes had completely come away from the other and the opening was well over a foot in diameter, exposing a dark tunnel into the plumbing system. I swore under my breath and peered inside, baffled as to how such a solid piece of pipe had come away and by how much space there was behind my walls; it was nearly enough for an entire new room. With a bubble of excitement, I entertained fantasies of expanding the bathroom. From inside the pipe, strange voices seem to bounce against the round walls of the metal tunnel. At first, I recoiled in fright. Then I became curious.

'*Beth.*'

On hearing my name, I leaned in further until my head was completely inside the dark metal tunnel. Whilst I could appreciate that there was no logic to my surroundings, there was a peculiar tug drawing me deeper.

'*Beth.*'

I wasn't imagining it. The walls of the pipe, although being absurdly large for bathroom pipes, were tight around my body as I shuffled further forward, manoeuvring my shoulders through its gaping mouth. Once my shoulders were inside, I edged forward and slithered along with ease. The walls on all sides of me were cold and slick, pushing me forward at an increasing speed, it occurred to me that the pipe was descending, and I was sliding down. I held my breath in anticipation before crying out at a particularly sudden drop.

All at once the voices came from all directions, echoing through the dark warren of plumbing, leaving me unsure if it was the strange voice, or just my own shouts bouncing off the walls. Placing my hands above me as the pipe levelled out and I stopped sliding, I felt the slippery metal over my head, hoping that I was the right way up. I once heard someone say that if you're in an avalanche you can become disorientated and end up digging deeper down when you try to get out, so you should spit to assess gravity. I spat into my hand and felt the saliva land warm in my palm. At least I knew I wouldn't be crawling deeper down into the maze of tunnels. Feeling the mouth of another pipe above me, I pulled myself up, gripping the small ledges where the pipes had been connected. An orb of light appeared and caused me to squint as I clambered higher. Once I reached it, I found my head slip through with ease, although it was too small for my shoulders to fit through as well. Glancing around, blinded by white porcelain, I realised that I was inside a Belfast sink. Straining to peer up over the edge, bright spotlights in the ceiling glimmered down over an immaculate kitchen. I instantly recognised the pastel décor and white marble. I was in Helen McIvor's kitchen. Somehow the plughole of her kitchen sink had expanded to allow my head to squeeze through.

I was distracted by an angry cry to my left. Twisting my head, I could see that Mrs McIvor was facing away from me, hurling eggs from a cardboard box at the wall. They shattered and left a rich orange yolk stain oozing down her white wall.

"Mrs Mc – Helen, are you all right?"

There was another scream. By the door, Mrs McIvor's teenage daughter Ella had clasped her hands over her mouth in horror and was pointing frantically at me.

"*Mum*!" She screamed. "Oh my God, Mum! There's a head coming out of the sink!"

An egg was fired in my direction, and I ducked instinctively, slipping back down the drain with an unpleasant squelch as the drain released me and contracted back into the size of an ordinary plughole. The orb of light above me became smaller until all that remained was a penny sized glow hovering over my head. My hands flailed wildly as I tried to scramble back up.

"*Helen*!" I called up. "It's me!"

There was a low rumble and then a rushing sound as the pipe began to fill with water, filling my mouth and nose as I spluttered in panic. The bitch had turned the taps on.

The force of the water pushed me back down to the main pipe which was gradually filling up. I scrambled breathlessly, wriggling as much as the restrictive space around me would allow. It felt suddenly smaller, as though the more I panicked, the tighter it became, retracting back to its natural size and constricting me in the process. Taking in a deep breath, I closed my eyes and submerged myself entirely, flexing my arms and swimming freely in the great, black, cavernous space which seemed to expand around me with my wave of calm.

Another orb of light glimmered up ahead and I kicked my legs to propel myself towards it. My head emerged into a dimly lit space as my hands grappled a round wooden seat that was about eye level. This time, I was in a toilet.

Blinking the water from my eyes, I examined my surroundings. A bathroom, a fancy one by my standards. It boasted a beautiful bronze slipper bathtub and gilt framed mirrors hanging from walls, bright and busy with decorative wallpaper. The bathroom door was open and out in the corridor I could make out a large, framed photograph on a small antique table. It was unmistakably Jeanie and her husband whose name I could either not recall or had never been told. Even in her photograph, she exuded a glossy glow, bright eyed and with the kind of smile you would never dream of trying to remove the crinkles from. I was in Jeanie's house.

I opened my mouth to shout for help as I began wriggling out of the toilet bowl, the pipe growing tight around my stomach. Before I had the chance to call out, I heard something.

A strange dragging sound came from the corridor, followed by heavy, ragged breathing. I shut my mouth, struck by an inexplicable realisation that something was very wrong.

'*Beth. Come back.*'

I heard the warning voice beneath me, back inside the pipes. Slinking back, I lowered myself down and felt the toilet water brush my chin.

'*Beth. Don't get out.*'

Through the open bathroom door, a hand with long spindly fingers appeared from behind the wall. My mouth fell open and I resisted the urge to scream as I watched the creature drag its body along, passing the bathroom door and making its way down the corridor. I inhaled sharply, ready to cry out and alert Jeanie to the monster in her house, but the voice urged me to keep quiet. As the creature continued to pull itself along, having not noticed me, a large dog with a honey-coloured coat padded alongside it, seemingly unperturbed. The creature was a grotesque amalgamation of human components, arms, legs, a torso and a head, both skinny and fat at the same time, with flesh hanging off bones that were of strange proportions. Wheezing heavily, it sloped passed me without turning.

'*Beth.*'

The voice became more insistent, summoning me back down. Taking another deep breath, I descended back down the toilet and into the pipes, heart pumping with adrenaline from the sight of the creature and making it more difficult to hold my breath.

Resisting the urge to inhale as I submerged myself further, I pulled myself forward through water that now seemed as thick as treacle. My fists hammered against the sides of the pipe, trying to find a way out as my lungs swelled against the tightness of my ribcage and my eyes stung from the pressure.

'*Beth.*'

After a moment, my hands found another opening above me and I crawled desperately into it, finding myself inside another pipe that descended sharply in another direction. Picking up speed, I slid downwards, water splashing around me and indicating that I wasn't fully submerged any more. I took a long, grateful breath as I was tossed out of the darkness, landing heavily on a concrete floor below.

I lay still for several moments, frightened in case I moved to find that something was broken. Gradually, I flexed my fingers, then my arms and legs and finally my back. Everything moved as it should have, save the cracking of joints which were stiff from the chill of the pipes. As my eyes adjusted to the low light, I made out a great cavernous space made from smooth concrete and in the shape of a tunnel. Troughs had been dug into the ground and water flowed rapidly by in narrow, artificial streams, like a sewer. Although I wasn't entirely sure what a sewer was supposed to look like, I felt certain they weren't normally as vast as this.

"Oh! Look, another one! I didn't realise that there was another one. Did you?"

"No. I don't recognise her, do you?"

"Yes – she lives in the clachan. It's Flora's daughter!"

"I didn't realise she was one of us."

I scrambled unsteadily to my feet and turned to the source of the voices. There was a large dinner table lined with long, white wax candles that created a warm orange orb of light. The surface was scattered with drinks, bottles, ashtrays, decks of cards and balls of wool. A group of women sat in the armchairs that surrounded it and stared at me silently. I instantly recognised several of them as the old women from the hamlet who knitted the alpaca wool jumpers; some of them were holding their knitting needles and had their balls of wool on their laps. Others, whom I didn't recognise, held books and smoked cigarettes while they lounged lazily in their chairs. Eventually, one of the old women from the hamlet placed down her needles and rose unsteadily to her feet, moving towards me with slow, shuffling movements.

"Plumbing." She murmured, stopping several feet away to examine me before looking up at the metal pipe that protruded up above through the tunnel ceiling. "That was an excellent idea! Tell me, did you shrink yourself or did you expand the pipes?"

"What?" I blinked and wrapped my arms around my body. Noticing me tremble, another woman immediately shuffled towards me with an oversized aquamarine wool jumper. She pulled it gently over my head and eased my arms through the sleeves without saying a word. The jumper emitted a warmth as though it had been plucked freshly from a radiator. I felt my sore, cold muscles sink gratefully inside it.

"Do you smoke?" She asked, taking a packet from her pocket and lit one before gesturing in my direction. I shook my head and she shrugged, moving back to her chair.

"*Well?*" The other woman looked impatiently at me, eyes sparkling with a youth that didn't match her aged body. "Did you shrink yourself or expand the pipes?"

"I have no idea what you're talking about." Shaking my head, I shrank deeper into the rolls of the jumper.

"To get down here of course, you travelled through the plumbing and the drains!" She grinned with teeth so perfect that they had to be false. "Poor Marion was digging for days before she found us, Linda followed rats through caves in the forest – and Eve here," she gestured at a younger and significantly more glamorous woman who I didn't recognise. Eve looked up at me with an intense stare and I noticed that one of her eyes was blue and the other brown. Beneath the thick alpaca wool jumper, she wore a fitted business suit that appeared to be covered in dirt. "Well, she planted herself in the ground and waited for her roots to find us! She used some poor lad as her fertiliser in order to help her grow down here!" The women around her all tutted and Eve lowered her head sadly, placing a hand against her stomach.

"I don't understand." I shook my head.

The women all frowned, glancing at each other uncertainly before one of them spoke.

"I don't think she knows."

"She must do – to have made it here, she must have known."

"She doesn't sound like she knows – maybe nobody ever told her."

"Dear," the woman approached me, placing a delicate, papery hand on my shoulder. "You felt it, didn't you? You felt it pull you, drawing you down here to be with us? Just like we all felt it."

"I," I paused hesitantly, "I heard voices in the pipes, I followed the voices down here."

"Interesting." She examined my face as though she was looking for lies. "So, you don't know why you're here?"

I shook my head.

"I see." The woman began to guide me towards one of the faded old armchairs that looked like one from my mother's house. "Why don't you take a seat, and then we can have a chat. Marion, pour the lassie a sherry."

"A chat about what?" My teeth began to chatter as a small tumbler was pressed into my hands.

"The end of the world." The woman replied simply.

THREE
BEDTIME STORIES

Polly

The little girl awoke to the sound of creaking pipes from the plumbing behind the walls. The house she lived in was old, and apparently pipes in old houses were noisy. Her old home had been in a tower in a city with lots of little box homes piled on top of one another. There, the pipes had been quiet, but the people were loud. Here, the people were always quiet.

Swinging her legs over the side of her bed, the girl glanced at the sparkly pink clock on her bedroom wall. In school she had been taught to read the time and the clock arms said that it was close to ten o'clock – the daytime one, not the night-time one. She used to be up much earlier than ten o'clock in the daytime, back when the nice old lady who smelt like lavender would come and collect her for school. She would wait at the door because Mummy didn't like having her inside the house and she would always smile at the girl and remind her to call her 'Nanny'. Lavender Nanny always told the girl wonderful stories on the drive to school and had said to her that if she tried hard enough, she could do or be anything she wanted.

The girl loved school. School was bright and cheery and filled with toys and loud noises; it was a place where the girl could be excited and run around until she was tired. At home, the girl was often told to be quiet because Mummy had a sore head. Since school had been closed, Lavender Nanny hadn't been over. The girl thought she recognised her voice distantly through the phone a few weeks ago but she could only make out little snippets.

'You just use me... I pay your rent... not my fault he's not there for you... poor wee lassie... stuck with a drunk like you... Just give her the phone for a minute, please Lisa... I love that girl you know.'

I love you too, Lavender Nanny, the girl thought to herself sadly.

Mummy was already awake and sitting at the kitchen table by the time the girl got up that morning, which was unusual. She looked nicer than she normally did, with her fair gingery hair straightened like a fine silk curtain over her shoulders and instead of her jogging bottoms she had figure hugging jeans which hung low and exposed a small white strip of stomach, lined with faint silvery marks. Although the girl thought she looked wonderful, Mummy would often complain that the girl had ruined her body. The girl didn't remember doing that, but Mummy wouldn't lie. The girl felt very guilty about it.

Thankfully, that morning Mummy was in an exceptionally good mood and sat at the table with a broad smile as she smoked her cigarette. There was a bottle of Dr Pepper and a clear glass bottle in front of her.

She gestured for the girl to come over, and ruffled her hair.

"I've decided enough is enough." Stubbing her cigarette out in the ashtray, she placed the girl on her lap. "We haven't had any fun lately with all that's going on." The girl nodded, as this was true. "So, we're not going to follow the rules any more."

The girl brightened, it was the rules that had stopped her from going to school or to the park, the rules that were made since things became strange.

"Does that mean we can go play in the park, Mummy?" When the girl spoke, she noticed the difference between her voice and Mummy's. Mummy often criticised the girl for having an American twang and said it was because she watched too much telly, but Mummy was the one who told the little girl to be quiet and watch the telly. It didn't make much sense.

"No." Mummy shook her head. "Don't want to get in trouble now – still have to be careful. Robbie's going to come visit!"

"Robbie." The girl mouthed the name. She remembered Robbie back from when they lived in the tower; that was before Lavender Nanny helped them move 'up north'. The girl had thought that up north would be deep in the snow, surrounded by reindeer and Christmas presents, but it wasn't like that at all. Back in the tower, in a place called Glasgow, Robbie had been in and out of their flat, sometimes laughing and sometimes shouting. Mummy called him *'unpredictable'*. The girl tried her best to like him, he was her daddy after all, but nobody really called him that, so the girl stuck with Robbie.

Mummy put the girl in the shower which, as usual, she hated at first. She whined at the stinging soap suds in her eyes and her cold, damp head. However, once it was over, her skin felt silky smooth and she could easily run her fingers through her orange ringlets without catching on any knots. She felt wonderful. Mummy let her wear her school pinafore and she pulled it over a pink jumper. The girl didn't especially like the colour pink, it made her think of a time she was sick after eating too many sweeties. Her favourite colour was green, green like the parks and the forests and the jungles she watched on the telly. She had been sad when all the ink had been used up in her green pen, so she had started colouring her trees in yellow. She learnt that if you carefully put blue over the top, it would make a colour that looked a little bit like her green.

Robbie arrived later that evening. He came through the back door and was ushered in quickly by Mummy, who glanced furtively from side to side.

"That bitch Helen will report me if she sees you here."

Robbie smirked.

"Report us to who? There's nobody left."

Robbie had a smile that the girl didn't like very much. His smile wasn't one that appeared if something funny had happened or if he was being kind, it stretched across one side of his face when he was thinking of something bad.

"How's my wee girl?" He asked, looking down at the girl but not bending down to her level. She looked up, her eyes meeting his protruding Adams apple. He looked different from the last time she had seen him; he had shaved off all his hair and his teeth didn't look like they fitted his face any more. The girl stared silently at him.

"She's shy." Mummy laughed.

Robbie shrugged and turned away to pick up a glass from the sink. Mummy poured.

"Crazy out there, eh?" He shook his stubbly head and took a long, grateful swig. "Roadblocks all over, people got this strange look about them, it's like there's something in the air – it's not right." Shuddering at the memory, he drained his glass and started to light a cigarette, his voice was muffled as his lips pursed around it. "I needed to get out of the city, thanks for having me." When the cigarette was lit, he passed it to Mummy and began lighting another one. Mummy smiled.

"Go watch telly." She shooed the girl with a wave of her hand.

"I've watched everything." The girl complained. Turning to her, Robbie raised an eyebrow and frowned.

"She's watched *everything*?"

"What else is there to do?" Mummy snapped defensively. "She's got one of those child lock things on the account, means she can only watch the kids' stuff."

"Aw, take that shite off. Then she'll have plenty to watch."

~

Adults watched some strange things. The girl flicked through the little boxes, taking her time to read the short descriptions promising a good story. A lot of grown-up telly seemed to be watching other grown-ups leading normal lives and having normal conversations. The girl couldn't fathom why anyone would be interested in that.

She stopped clicking when she reached a box with a picture of people in strange green metallic outfits and big bubble helmets. They stood in front of a backdrop of stars and planets. It looked like fun. As the music from the kitchen became louder and Mummy started to make her shrieking laugh after everything Robbie said, the girl turned the volume up and furrowed her brow in concentration at the telly. Much of the storyline didn't make sense to her, but she loved all the stars and the planets, and she particularly liked the ship captain who was so brave and funny. She laughed aloud with him and his crew as they chuckled together on their spaceship adventures.

There were several films with the kind spaceman. That evening, the girl watched every single one and she didn't fall asleep until it was two o'clock in the night-time, which was technically morning even though the girl knew it was still night. Unable to keep her eyes open any longer, she sank into the sofa as the lights went out and Mummy and Robbie retired to bed.

~

The girl awoke to a gentle knocking on the living room window. Rubbing her bleary eyes, she saw a strange blue light shining in from outside, partially blocked by the outline of a man whose curled knuckles were rapping against the glass. Sliding warily off the sofa, she approached him. His head was hugely oversized compared to his long, smooth body. As she looked closer, she realised that the oversized head was actually a helmet. Her hands struggled with the latch on the window before tugging it out and letting it swing open. Her face was struck by a pleasantly cool breeze in contrast to the muggy summer air, it came from a large glass and steel contraption that was whirring behind the man. He removed his helmet and extended his hand.

"Good evening Polly!" He said brightly.

Polly. That was what they called her in school.

"It's you!" She gasped, clasping the spaceman's large hand tightly in hers.

"Sure is." He beamed a perfect, white-toothed smile. "You fancy helping us out on tonight's mission? Our navigator called in sick and we thought we'd have to call the whole thing off, but then we heard you might be interested?"

The girl gasped, feeling her heart bounce about gleefully in her chest.

"*Yes!*" She cried.

Behind the spaceman, the crew began filing down the ramp, cheering for her in whispers, which the girl was grateful for since she wouldn't want them to wake up Mummy or Robbie. The spaceman took her hand and led her up the steel ramp while the crew high fived her as she passed. At the door of the egg-shaped contraption, the girl's eyes widened in wonder.

"The landing pod!"

"You know your stuff, Polly." The spaceman gestured for her to go inside.

As the pod rumbled into action, the girl strapped herself in beside the spaceman and they braced themselves for take-off. The girl could feel her cheeks dragging down from the speed of the ascent as the sky went from being a soft grey blue to navy, and then to an inky black, before an explosion of glittering stars appeared around them. Down below, the Earth sparkled in rich blues and greens with whirls of white spiralling across land and oceans.

The girl felt tears prick her eyes, but she wasn't sure why.

The landing pod clicked into place, connecting with a larger ship that was the shape of a fat, wingless airplane. Inside, it buzzed with activity from shiny screens and rows of polished, colourful controls.

"Thanks so much for this, Polly." The spaceman patted her shoulder firmly before hanging up his helmet and suit, revealing a green spandex uniform underneath. He tossed the girl one of the green suits which she wriggled into with ease.

"No problem." The girl beamed, taking her seat in front of the ship's window which spanned wide and looked out over bright orbs of planets, some surrounded by neat rings and others glimmering with activity. It was dizzying.

"Crew ready?" The spaceman sat down beside her and glanced behind him.

"Just about!" A beautiful woman with bright red hair approached the girl and placed a steaming mug of hot chocolate and plate of chocolate biscuits on the surface next to her. The woman smiled, exuding warmth. "Now we're ready, Captain."

That night, they travelled through the stars together. The girl steered the ship and navigated them through asteroid fields with ease. Sometimes she chose to fly at lightspeed, taking great pleasure in watching everything blur around her and hearing the excitable whoops of the crew. Other times, she stopped the ship altogether, just so she could look out over the great expanse of outer space. She laughed alongside the crew as they ate their biscuits and sipped on the richest hot chocolate she had ever tasted, as if pure chocolate had been melted in the mug.

When the mission was complete, they bundled into the landing pod and descended to Earth, landing in the girl's back garden. She felt a sharp pang of sadness that reminded her of the day Nanny Lavender had stopped taking her to school. She resisted the urge to beg them to let her stay, after all, that never worked. Instead, recalling one of the scenes from the film, she straightened herself up and clasped the spaceman's hand in hers.

"I will never forget you." She said clearly, blinking back a tear.

"Nor will I forget you, Polly." He touched her cheek with his warm hand and paused. They stood silently for a moment that the girl would cherish for all her days. Then, releasing her hand, he retreated back to his crew who stood by the landing pod door and simultaneously saluted her, eyes glittering against the low light of the early dawn. The girl returned the salute before crawling back through the window and tiptoeing to her bedroom where she removed her suit, put on her pink pyjamas and crept into bed.

~

"Oh Mummy, it was *wonderful*!" The girl spoke through a mouthful of sugary cereal flakes straight from the packet and waved her free hand around her to emphasise the point. "Sometimes I flew so fast that planets went *whizz* right past me!"

"Christ's sake Lisa," Robbie nursed his temples and pulled a face. "Does that kid ever shut up?"

"Shut it," Mummy snapped, blowing out an icing sugar plume from her cigarette. It drifted round the kitchen in a strange grey fug. The girl frowned and tried to chew her cereal as quietly as possible. Moments later, she was ushered out by Mummy and placed in front of the telly with the remote. Sighing wearily, the girl was disappointed to remember that she had finished all the spaceman films the previous day.

There were other options for space films, but some of them looked quite scary and the girl didn't want to be frightened. Instead, she clicked on one with castles and dragons. It was quite good. There were princesses weighed down by jewels and gowns, and wizards in cloaks who wielded great wooden staffs as they cast spells. The wizards had powerful, booming voices that made entire kingdoms tremble beneath them.

That evening, the girl returned to her room after Mummy had told her to turn off the telly because her and Robbie were having an early night. Neither of them looked very well and the girl figured that Robbie must have caught Mummy's sore head. She hoped she didn't catch it too.

The girl played with her dolls until she was too tired and then dragged them over to the toybox at the end of her bed. She opened the lid and peered inside.

"Princess Polly!"

The girl gasped and jumped back as an old man in a dark grey cloak untangled his spindly limbs and clambered from the toybox. Reaching down, he pulled out a long grey staff that shouldn't have fitted in there. Smoothing his wispy white beard, he cleared his throat.

"Princess Polly, your majesty." He bowed his head low. "I am so glad to have finally found you."

"A *princess*?" The girl's eyes widened.

"Yes, and I am your loyal advisor, wizard of the kingdom, here to take you back to your rightful home." Reaching back into the toybox, he pulled out a bright pink dress, handfuls of sparkling jewels and finally, a glittering diamond crown. The girl frowned.

"What does a princess do?" She asked.

"Why, she rules her kingdom of course!" The wizard chuckled. "And she is loved by all."

"Hmm." She girl paused thoughtfully. "I think I'd rather be a wizard."

There was a moment of silence and the wizard let out a deep belly laugh.

"But you're a princess!"

"Well in that case, you must obey me." The girl snapped, narrowing her eyes. "I want to be a wizard and *you* will teach me magic."

~

"And he taught me how to cast spells and we fought dragons!" The girl followed Mummy and Robbie into the kitchen that morning. "And we were invited to a magical party at the palace where the queen told me how proud she was of me and how brave I had been! I even got a crown, it's in my room, do you want to see?"

Robbie rose to his feet. There was an unpleasant glistening grey sheen to his face. Snatching the girls arm roughly, he tossed her out into the corridor wordlessly and slammed the kitchen door. Muffled shouts ensued on the other side and the girl heard something smash.

Back in front of the telly, the girl snuffled, rubbing the sore area where Robbie had grabbed her arm. She clicked on the first box she saw. It was horrible. The film started off with normal people, but then suddenly they were being hunted during the night by other people with sharp teeth and pale faces. They called themselves vampires and they drained bodies dry, littering the streets with shrivelled corpses. Trembling, the girl hid behind her pillow. She wasn't sure what frightened her more, the vampires, or the screaming and banging that was coming from the kitchen.

~

"*Polly.*" The voice was slippery and smooth as it drifted through her bedroom that night. "*Polly.*"

A shadow spread across her room, making the dark figure approaching her bed seem bigger than it actually was. The girl clenched her duvet and whimpered.

"Go away!"

The dark outline paused at the foot of her bed, breathing softly for several moments before speaking again.

"I'm not here to hurt you, Polly." It whispered. "I'm here to ask you to join us. Don't you want to be strong and powerful like us?"

"I *am* strong and powerful!" The girl insisted. "I'm a spaceman *and* a wizard!"

"Spacemen and wizards don't live forever, Polly." It approached the bed with slow, purposeful steps. "Don't you want to live forever, Polly?"

The girl hesitated for just a moment before nodding.

"Yes." She breathed, as the darkness descended upon her.

~

"What the hell is she doing still in bed?" Mummy banged on the door the following evening, having only just noticed that the girl had not been up all day. She twisted the handle sharply and kicked it open.

"Fuck sake Lisa, stop shouting." Robbie barked. "My head is killing me."

"It's her! She hasn't been out of bed all day!"

Robbie eyes rolled in their gaunt sockets and he marched into the room, snatching the corner of the duvet.

"*Oi!*" He barked. "Get up, lazy girl!"

He whipped the pink duvet back and beneath it, the girl lay very still as she looked up at him. His eyes widened in surprise as he looked at her.

"My name is *Polly*."

Polly wore a dark grey cloak over a metallic green onesie and a diamond crown atop her head of orange curls. A wooden staff was clasped between her small hands and pressed against her chest. Her lips stretched into a wide smile to reveal her pointed teeth.

Robbie and Mummy began to scream.

~

By all standards, it was a pleasant evening, and Polly knew that even though it was dark there was nothing to be afraid of any more. As she stepped outside her front door and prepared to walk into the woods, she glanced at the house next door. The witch they called Beth was standing by her bathroom window staring at her with sad grey eyes. Mummy had always said that the witch was a '*strange woman*' and told Polly not to speak to her. '*She's a creepy witch*', Mummy would say. The witch rarely came outside, and, when she did, her hair was tangled and her clothes hung loose like unflattering rags from her pudgy body. Polly used to be afraid knowing that a witch lived next door, but the wizard had told her that, contrary to the storybooks, most witches weren't bad, they were often just lonely. Polly waved at her.

The witch waved back, offering a small, sad smile. Pausing, Polly remembered that it was the duty of a princess to ensure that the people of her kingdom were happy, so she whispered words that the wizard had taught her and pointed her staff in the witch's direction.

"You poor old witch, you look so drained. Here's a little magic to help you on your way – go find the other witches and be happy." She said, even though she knew that the witch couldn't hear her.

Turning to the forest, Polly paused thoughtfully, watching as a man wearing a sheepskin coat flitted past her without noticing her presence. She recognised him as the neighbour that the women of her kingdom hated; they called him a pest, and Polly instinctively knew that he was entering the forest with wicked intentions. So, without hesitating, she slipped into the trees and followed him through the darkness. After all, it was a princess's duty to protect her kingdom.

FOUR
EVERYTHING MUST SPARKLE

Helen

VIDEO 1

"Hi, viewers, my name is Helen McIvor. It's *so* nice to see so many folk following me – it means a lot, particularly in these *strange* times. I thought I'd start making these videos as a little distraction – especially now so many of us are stuck at home and not working.

I admit it, I'm *so* lucky to live where I do, in a little hamlet in the countryside close to the shore. It's beautiful and all my neighbours are just wonderful, there's a real sense of community which I *love*. There's our little cluster of houses and then it's just rolling hills and sparkling shorelines for miles – it really is idyllic, and there's also the city – just a small one – a few miles away so we aren't too isolated.

Anyway, this whole thing has been pretty hard on me in spite of where I live and all the friends I have. It's been particularly frustrating with all this beautiful weather we've been having – I mean honestly, hot weather in the High-lands is a real rarity and the one time we get it, this happens! I'm normally *such* a sociable person too, I love spending time with my family, I have a wonderful husband Paul and two *gorgeous* kids: Ella, she's seventeen, and Rachel, she's six. Quite the age gap, I know – what was I thinking, haha.

What was I saying? Oh yeah, socialising. So, when I'm not with my family I'm normally out with friends. I formed this little book club with the other mums from the parent teacher association at Rachel's school – really, it's more a wine club, but *shh*! Paul wouldn't approve. I do a lot with our local church, I organise bake sales, picnics – ugh, this weather would be *perfect* for picnics – etcetera, etcetera. I *love* cooking and baking; I love organising things too. Now, I know what you're thinking: '*how can organising be a hobby?*' But it is! Sometimes when I'm really stressed out, I like to go into the kitchen – my favourite room in our house – and I'll just spend the day going through the cupboards sorting everything out. The kids keep me busy. Honestly, when they put away the shopping it is an absolute nightmare, I'm telling you.

My friends are always saying to me *'oh Helen, you need to write a cookbook, or start an Instagram for all your beautiful baking, or do a lifestyle blog'* and to be honest, before all this I was always too busy to give it much thought. Being a mum and a housewife is a full-time job. Paul's away a lot, so it's really important for me to spend as much time with the kids as possible so that we can –

'Mum, where's the TV remote?'

Sorry everyone, this is my daughter Ella. Ella sweetheart, you know we don't watch the television during the day.

'But Mum, I'm so bored. There's literally nothing to do.'

There is *always* something to do. Go read a book, maybe you could help around the house a bit more. Don't you give me that look!

Sorry! Poor Ella's been so grumpy of late, not being able to see her friends is really taking its toll. We're home-schooling at the moment – although, I have Ella doing the curriculum for the year ahead already – but my goodness, does that girl rebel. Teenagers!

So where was I, yes, so when the announcement was made that we should all be staying at home and all the shops were shut, my first instinct was obviously to panic. I mean, they didn't even tell us what was going on – but I suppose there are some things that we're better off not knowing, isn't that right? Anyway, stressing out doesn't get you anywhere, so I figured I *had* to do something to keep me sane. So, I'm going to make a short video each week or so, just with little hints and tips for cooking, baking, cleaning – and just generally how to keep your home looking and feeling lovely! In my house, everything *must* sparkle.

I think that it's *so* important in these strange times that we strive to keep ourselves and our surroundings looking and feeling as good as possible. But before we get started on the hard stuff, I can't stress how important it is to take care of yourself first. Given that I think we all need something to brighten our day, there's no better way of doing this than having a bit of 'me time'. All you need is a sit down with a piece of cake and a hot, fresh coffee – get on a video call to your friends and have a gossip, maybe take the time to catch up with your kids – Ella sweetie, do you fancy helping me with the –

'No.'

Or you can just have a few minutes to yourself. So today I'm going to share my secret Bakewell slice recipe – a big shout-out to my newest neighbour Jeanie who paid me the *biggest* compliment when I went over with a hamper of them to welcome her to the hamlet – she said that they were the *best* Bakewell slices she had *ever* eaten – and Jeanie is from the city so you can bet she's been to all the best bakeries!

The first step is the shortcrust pastry. Before you start *please* ensure that you have baking beans to hand so you don't get any of those nasty lumps and bumps…"

VIDEO 2

"Hey viewers, I hope you've all been keeping well. It's been a particularly tough week for me as this weather is just getting increasingly glorious – but can I please remind everyone that the guidance is to stay inside and I've noticed a few folk going for a walk or a little jog – I appreciate how tempting that must be, but I can't emphasise how important it is that we all follow the guidance. I've been hearing some crazy stories about what's going on out there, you know it's funny, you can almost feel that there's something wrong in the air. I'm doing my best to ignore it.

I'm finding it really helps to sit in my glass conservatory which looks out over the sea – I *adore* the way the sunlight sparkles against the cool crisp water, it just makes me want to throw on my bathing suit and jump right in! My kids often complain that it's a stony beach rather than a sandy one – but I think that's so much better. Who wants messy sand between your toes that you drag into the house and get it stuck in your clothes? *Yuck*. With smooth pebbles there's no mess at all!

So anyway, with the beginning of summer well and truly rolling in, I am *so* far behind with my annual spring clean! An immaculate house *always* makes me feel better, and the best part is, it can be fun for all the family! I've got the kids here to help me today, say hi kids!

'Hi.'

I always think that the best place to start is the kitchen but that's because it's my favourite room in the house. However, you might be different so start with what feels right for you. If the living room is more your thing, then please do feel free to start there. Once you've done your favourite room, I always find that it spurs me on to do the rest of the house – even the rooms you hate! For example, I *hate* doing the kids rooms –

'Mum, I don't want you to clean my room. I've told you this so many times.'

Shh, Ella. But what I can't stress enough is that you do all the rooms with hard flooring and porcelain surfaces together, since you're going to need bleach for that. It's better you do it all at once to avoid exposing yourself to those nasty chemicals too much.

Ella! Why does Rachel have the bleach?

'Because you told her to wipe down the skirting boards?'

Oh my Lord, Ella – not with bleach! You do *not* give a small child bleach – have you any idea of the damage it could do to my woodwork?"

VIDEO 3

"Hi everyone, so I know it's really early, but I wanted to be up first thing. Now that your houses are sparkling clean, it's time to get started with some proper cooking so you can delight your family with fantastic meals! So, let's get those gleaming cupboards stocked up with lovely ingredients.

Most of my neighbours order their shopping from the big chain supermarkets for delivery but I prefer not to do that. I much prefer to order from our local butcher, fishmonger and greengrocer. Some of them have managed to start a delivery service which, although it costs way more, is absolutely worth it! Since things got strange, they have these special armoured vans – I think they cost quite a lot which is why they have to charge so much now. I can't stress how important it is to buy local where you can, it keeps small businesses running, particularly in these tough times and it's so much better for the environment. Even for Rachel's birthday this year, instead of ordering off some big online retailer like I might have done in the past, I'm getting a local artist to commission a dollhouse for her – she is going to be *thrilled*.

So here I am, standing by my gate – still technically *in* my home! I'm waiting for the delivery driver to show up, but while I'm here I'm going to take a quiet moment to myself to watch that beautiful sparkling sea over the road. It's magnificent, isn't it? It's times like these that you really have to appreciate the simple things in life.

Dum, dum dum… A little later than usual, but hey ho.

Oh! Here he is! Morning!

(the sound of a van rumbling up the drive)

Oh – where's Billy?

'He won't be doing deliveries any more. Ma'am, can I please ask you to go back into your house.'

What? Why?

'I'm not getting out of this van until I can see that there's nobody outside. I'll put the goods on the ground by the gate and you can come get them once I've driven away.'

Oh, ok, Billy normally just –

'As I said, Billy won't be doing deliveries any more.'''

(video cuts out)

"Well, that was weird! To be honest with you, I haven't really been keeping up with the news so much. I follow the advice on the telly and the radio and that's about it as far as I'm concerned. There hasn't been a new announcement in some time, but I assume that's because nothing has changed yet. As I've said before, we don't really know what's going on, but I refuse to listen to these nonsense conspiracy theories – you know – oh it's the end of the world – aliens have landed – comets have passed over the Earth so close that the gravitational pull is off balance – haha, such nonsense. Honestly, it'll be all witches and fairy tales next. I have this neighbour, Matthew the p – Matthew, I noticed he has this browny red message he's drawn on his door window that says 'CAN'T TRUST ANY OF THEM' – I reckon he's one of those conspiracy theorists, he's gone and smashed his other window too! I swear, at this rate his place will be as bad as Beth's. I haven't seen Matthew in a couple of days, he's probably sitting in his washing cupboard with a walkie-talkie and a tin foil hat – haha. Not that it's any of my business, but I did see a woman through his window just a couple of weeks ago! She was wearing this beautiful suit, although if I'm being perfectly honest it was desperately in need of a good iron. She was actually quite pretty, too. Perhaps a girlfriend will be good for him. I hope she knows what she's getting herself into – oh I should stop, I'm not normally one to gossip like this!

For dinner tonight, I will be making my duck egg and asparagus salad with crisp Parma ham. It's always a crowd pleaser – and it's so darn simple too! The trick to boiling the egg to perfection, is to have it on the rolling boil for just under the time you'd expect for an egg to be of that nice creamy consistency and then take it out and immediately drop it into ice cold water and let it continue to cook inside the shell while it cools, you end up with this gorgeous jammy orange yolk that is just *divine*. The only thing worse than an undercooked yolk is an overcooked one, where the yolk takes that yellow powdery consistency. *Yuck*.

What on earth! These aren't duck eggs! That idiot gave me chicken eggs – Billy would never have mixed that up! This can't be happening.

'Mum, it tastes the same.'

My Lord Ella, you horrify me at times. These are no good!

'Mum – stop!'

Ridiculous!

(the sound of smashing against the wall)

'*Mum!*'

It's all *ruined*!

(the sound of screaming)
'Oh my God, Mum! There's a head in the sink!'"
(video cuts out)

"Evening everyone! Thought I ought to make a quick addendum to my video, following this morning's debacle! That was *so* silly, haha. As you can see, my salad turned out absolutely fine with the chicken eggs, although I would still recommend duck eggs for that meatier taste.

'Mum, what is the matter with you? You're scaring us.'

It's always been so important for me that a family enjoys their meals round the dinner table with one another.

'Mum will you please just look back at the video, you'll see it – there was a head in the sink!'

Ella dear, there's nothing wrong with my video. Anyway, as I was saying, I was brought up in a family who shared those same values, and it was always a time for me and my family to share stories of our day and catch up on what we'd all been up to. Of course, tonight poor Paul is still at work, so we have an empty chair at the table. Can't be helped!

'Mum, Dad left you ages ago.'

Ella.

'What the fuck is wrong with you?'
(the sound of silverware clattering on the table)

I've had quite enough of you, young lady. That mouth of yours needs to be washed out with soap.

'Get off me!'"

VIDEO 4

"Hi again viewers. I hope you've all been keeping your homes sparkling with the help of my handy hints. I know how hard it can be with kids, mine have been a bit of a handful lately – but I think I know why. As I recall saying in one of my earlier videos, in these strange times that we live in, it's *so* important to take the time to enjoy the simple things in life and with all these phones and screens everywhere, how are kids supposed to do that? It's constant visual stimulation that nobody needs right now. So, I've thrown out the televisions and all of our electronics – other than my iPad so that I can keep making these videos, of course. Ella's been a bit difficult about relinquishing her phone, but that's teenagers for you!"

VIDEO 5

"Viewers, I am so excited to finally introduce you to my husband Paul! I'm sorry, I know it's late, but Paul works such crazy hours these days – darling, are you hungry?

'Helen, where are the kids?'

'Dad! Thank God you're here!'
'Daddy!'
'Get in the car, both of you.'
Paul? What are you doing? *Paul?*"

VIDEO 6

"Hi everyone, so with Paul and the kids away on a little break, it's given me the time to get everything *really* sparkling and organised for when they get back. I can't wait to share all my more complex recipes with you now that I have the time on my hands! With the kids around it's just a bit much getting round to them.

I cannot *believe* the amount of rubbish Ella has lying about in her room – our garden is now piled high with all her useless junk. She has *so* many bags of makeup and I was absolutely *disgusted* to look inside and see the state of it all. Eyeshadow powder *everywhere* and her lipsticks looked like they'd been bludgeoned! As soon as she's back, I'm going to buy her some nice new makeup and teach her how to use it properly. I always ensure to wipe down the little containers after use and store them in tidy little compartments in my bathroom – speaking of which, I'm going to need to sort out the bathroom shortly. When I was looking in the mirror this morning, I noticed some out of place freckles on my nose, so I had to remove the mirror from the wall and smash it on the floor.

When you're feeling really overwhelmed, it's like I said before, just take a few minutes to yourself. I'm standing out in the garden trying to enjoy the sunshine, but the garden is *such* a mess with all that rubbish that I've chucked out of the house. I really wanted to do a video on gardening sometime soon, but this just won't do! The more I look at everything, it's all *such* a mess! I don't know how I didn't see it before, all the hedges are different sizes, the trees at unmatching heights – Matthew's broken door panel and over in strange Beth's house there are actually tiles missing from her roof! I'm not even surprised to be honest, that woman has no standards. There's overgrown grass and chipped paint on the doors. Perhaps I ought to just burn it all down, haha.

The only thing that I can see that looks perfect is that sparkling sea in the distance, flat and calm, like glass reflecting the bright, white sunlight and the baby blue of the clear afternoon sky – it's as close to heaven as I can imagine. It's *perfect*! I don't know why I never thought of this before – I will live in the sea!

Whoops – always look right and left before you cross the road. I still do that, more out of habit now that there are hardly any cars on the road, haha.

Ugh, my phone keeps vibrating in my pocket – who's calling me? *Robyn Hendrie*? Not now Robyn.

(the sound of metal and glass crunching against the ground)

Oh, it's so *wonderfully* crisp and cold against my feet as I stand on smooth pebbles. The sea will strip away any dirt from my body that was carried in the air. I will never need to smell any of those smells that I dislike so much ever again – after all, you can't smell anything under the water. My limbs will lengthen as I descend, and my toes and my fingers will web in perfect symmetry to allow me to swim down further and faster. My clean hair will unfurl from my ponytail and drift with the movement of the water. I will descend so deep that I am submerged in total darkness, and I will never have to witness mess or imperfection *ever* again. Paul and the kids will join me when they are ready, and sometimes, when the sun shines brightly enough through the water, we will turn on our backs and face away from the ocean floor. We will look up in awe, and *everything will sparkle*."

FIVE
GROUNDED

Eve

Eve sat in the business lounge at the airport with a large glass of wine from the open bar. Settling into one of the comfier armchairs, she took a deep breath and slipped her work phone and laptop back into her hand luggage. Her boss had left that morning on a flight for London where she was supposed to meet him later that afternoon, however her flight had been delayed. Instead of panicking, Eve took herself to the nicest airport lounge that the company expenses would allow. Eve had never been one to panic; after all, she was going to be late for the meeting whether she stressed or not. If she had no control over a situation, she refused to let stress or anxiety get the better of her; it was what made her so good at her job.

That was why it was so surprising when, suddenly, Eve felt an unfamiliar jolt of panic that clenched her stomach, just as her delayed flight appeared on the board with the gate number. Her eyes flickered around the lounge where the frequent fliers, harassed businessmen and wealthy holiday makers were either leisurely drinking or concentrating on paperwork and laptop screens. The young, bearded barman looked bored as he nodded his head to the beat of the music.

Without any explanation, Eve knew that none of the planes that took off that day would ever land and that none of the passengers would ever be seen or heard from again. Although, nobody else knew that yet.

Staring up at the screen that directed her to the gate, Eve tried to reason with herself. She wasn't prone to being irrational and she certainly didn't have any apprehensions when it came to flying since she was in the sky most weeks. Yet, every inch of her body was screaming at her not to board that flight and to get out. A strange pulling sensation in her gut tugged desperately, forcing her to rise to her feet. Slipping her phone back out of her bag, she decided to call her boss, Jeremy, an officious man who didn't like to be bothered unless it was absolutely necessary. He ought to have landed over an hour ago so she would call him to dispel her irrational panic.

The phone didn't ring.

"*Shit*." Eve breathed. Beads of perspiration had formed around her upper lip, salty and unpleasant. She glanced from side to side, finding something unnerving about the general air of calm in the lounge. None of them could sense that something terrible was happening.

She snatched her bag from the floor and marched out of the lounge, abandoning her suitcase that had already boarded the plane as she strode out the automatic doors of the airport with her stiletto heels clip-clopping at a slightly faster rate than usual. If she had stayed any longer, she would have noticed that the airport staff were starting to look anxious, whispering into their radios as they tried their best not to panic the passengers.

Getting into her car, she drove out of the airport carpark and called one final number.

"Hello?" Her assistant David always sounded nervous when she called him unexpectedly. She had hired him for his meticulous nature, but with it came excess angst.

"David, hi. It's Eve." Even in her panic, Eve managed to assume her authoritative business voice that had leaked into her personal life over the years. "Look, have you left the hotel yet?"

"Not yet." He replied uncertainly. "Why? I can leave now if you want -"

"*No.*" Eve interrupted sharply. "Listen to me *very* carefully David, I don't want you going anywhere near the airport. I can't explain it right now, but I want you to book another night in your hotel – more if needs be, and if anyone questions it just say that I authorised it. Okay?"

"Okay, but –"

"And don't leave the hotel."

"Sure. Eve, is everything all right?" Behind his fraught nippiness, David had a wonderful warmth about him that manifested in a genuine concern for others. It was what Eve really liked about him, although she would never have admitted it.

"I don't know yet."

"Where are you?"

"I'm just a bit outside Edinburgh." She replied, weaving onto the motorway. "But I'm heading up to a property I own in the Highlands."

"Why?"

"I don't know," she replied, which was entirely true. She remained uncertain as to why she would want to visit the shitty little investment property that a pushy family member and amateur financial advisor had pressed her into buying a couple of years back. However, it was impossible for her to ignore the tugging sensation in her belly that drew her there. Eve had always baffled her colleagues by knowing things before they happened, they said it was spooky. "Goodbye David, you take care of yourself now."

~

Several hours later, after countless wrong turns and numerous traffic diversions, Eve's car rumbled into a small hamlet in the north of Scotland. On paper, the place was perfect. Wedged comfortably between dense forestry and glittering shoreline, it afforded jagged mountain views, and it was only a short drive from Inverness so had none of the downsides that came with being too rural. Unfortunately, the property she bought had required more work than she anticipated. Radon sumps needed to be installed at a hefty cost and woodworm needed treated. Eventually Eve had simply handed it over to a letting agent who handled all the issues and sent her the bill. On the plus side, her latest tenant was a plumber so most of the recent issues had been handled 'in-house', so to speak.

As Eve parked up by the curb, she stepped out onto the dark street. She was surprised to find that there were no streetlamps, which made her feel suddenly vulnerable, a feeling that Eve was not accustomed to. The air around her had an unpleasant mugginess to it, clawing at her throat and preventing her from taking a full breath. She had been on business trips in the north of Scotland in the past and one of the things she had liked the most about it was the crisp, clean air that inflated her lungs and stripped her of the city pollution. Holding her hands out and stretching her palms, there was a static to the air that she couldn't explain, it rippled over her dry skin like a current. Eve shuddered, perturbed.

Slinging her tote over her shoulder, Eve clip-clopped down the narrow pavement and swung open the little white gate of her modest bungalow. There had been fancier newbuilds erected since she had last visited, all with groomed lawns and meticulously tended to flower boxes.

Holding her breath, Eve hesitated only for a moment at the green front door before knocking her clenched fist against a long, narrow glass panel. There was a moment of rustling and fussing behind the door and she squinted at the figure behind the frosted glass. Seconds later, it swung open. A man who looked to be in his late thirties or early forties answered. He would have been tall but, with the height of Eve's heels, he was at eye level with her. Despite the heat, he was wearing a thick sheepskin jacket, and his hair was ruffled as though he had just woken up.

"Can I help you?" He looked at her curiously, eyes examining the snug business suit and flickering to the expensive car parked on his drive next to his battered 4x4.

"Look," Eve adopted her formal tone again. "This is going to sound strange, but I'm the owner of this property – your landlady, technically. My name is Eve Sutherland and if you like, I can call my solicitor to get them to verify that. I would like to stay here if that's all right with you. I have no intention of evicting you or anything of the sorts – I just need to be here for the time being. I'll pay you double whatever it is you pay in rent, and I'll pay weekly. Does that sound fair?"

The man stared blankly at her for several seconds before blinking back to the present.

"You know," he said slowly, "there was a news announcement that just came out, saying we should all stay inside. Something weird is going on, you know that, right?"

I knew it, Eve thought triumphantly.

"Yes," she nodded, "I knew that."

Furrowing his brow thoughtfully, the man eventually shrugged and gestured for her to come inside. Eve stepped into a tidy but sparse white corridor.

"Well, double rent sounds more than fair to me," he said. "And who could say no to the company of a beautiful lady such as yourself." Smiling with a charmingly boyish grin, he held out his hand. "I'm Matthew, by the way."

~

Eve shut the bedroom door behind her and emptied her tote on the bed. Matthew explained that he had rented out the spare room briefly, technically against the terms of his lease, but Eve wasn't in a position to raise that. Like the rest of the house, it was clean but minimal. There was a single bedside table, a small dresser and a bare light bulb that swung from the ceiling. Had she not seen the rest of the house, she might have thought that the bare light bulb was intentional, in a kind of industrial chic way.

Her purse, passport, airline tickets, makeup bag, laptop and two books scattered the white duvet. That, along with her car, was all she had. It wasn't until Eve sat down on the edge of the bed that she realised how exhausted she was. Her neck ached from the long drive and her eyelids felt heavy. The peculiar pull in her stomach had eased off slightly, as though recognising her exhaustion and allowing her to rest. Pulling her cropped hair from the professional updo, she let the dark bangs brush her cheeks and peeled off her restrictive skirt and suit jacket. Folding them carefully and placing them on the dresser, she flopped back on the bed in her underwear, too hot to get beneath the duvet as she drifted into a dreamless sleep. When she awoke the following morning, she was mortified to see that the door had swung open, and she hoped that Matthew hadn't walked by at any point during the night.

~

"You look stressed," Matthew commented one morning as Eve was sat at the breakfast bar. He placed a plate of toast with butter and raspberry jam in front of her, as he had taken to doing each morning since Eve had arrived on his doorstep. The small act of kindness made Eve smile up at him as she nursed her mug of coffee.

"I haven't heard from work in a whole week." Clunking her phone irritably on the wooden work surface, Eve frowned at the screen. "I don't know what's going on. Nobody's picking up."

Matthew watched her curiously, taking a bite of his toast.

"I think there are bigger issues than your work right now." Matthew gestured at the television screen which showed the same white message against a black screen as it had every day since Eve had arrived. STAY AT HOME. They had kept the television on just in case it changed.

"No, I *know* that." Eve replied rattily. "Sorry, I'm just frustrated. I don't think I've ever stayed in the same place for more than a few days at a time since I was young. It makes me edgy."

"Really?"

"Obviously I have a flat, but I'm hardly ever there. I'm always travelling with work." Eve was babbling, something she rarely did. "I live out of a suitcase in hotels – and when I'm in the city, I'm usually in the office. My flat never really felt like a home, just a place to sleep sometimes."

"Hmm," Matthew looked thoughtful. "That sounds tiring."

"I'm always tired," she said quickly, "but then, I'm one of those live to work types rather than a work to live. I saw this psychiatrist once when things were really busy with the company and I wasn't getting any sleep – he recommended that I take some time off, but I knew that would stress me out more. A prescription for diazepam did the trick and I was back on my feet after a good night's sleep."

"Jesus, Eve." Laughing, Matthew finished his breakfast and began tidying away both his and Eve's breakfast dishes. He gestured at the coffee machine and Eve nodded, handing him her empty mug. "Sounds like you need a break. Tell you what, why don't I make you dinner tonight? Leave your phone somewhere else and we'll have a nice meal, a bottle of wine and play some scrabble or something – we can forget whatever crap is going on in the world right now, whether it be your work or the apocalypse?"

Eve paused.

"Come on Eve, I've watched you living off plain pasta and toast all week."

"I'm not used to cooking." She replied tartly.

"It wasn't a criticism; I'm trying to be nice." He smiled his boyish grin.

"Well," she hesitated briefly, "can we play chess instead of scrabble?"

"Absolutely."

Eve returned the smile and nodded.

"All right then. It's a date."

~

Leaning forward, Matthew refilled Eve's glass as she twirled the spaghetti round her fork. Once full, he leaned back, waiting tentatively as she took her first bite.

"Matthew, this is *amazing*. Where did you learn to cook like this?" She gestured at the plate of seafood and pasta, holding out her hands which were messy from shelling prawns.

"It's normally better." He feigned modesty. "With everywhere shut, I'm just ordering my seafood frozen from the supermarket fishmonger – when things get better and I can get my hands on better ingredients, then I'll show you how good it can really be."

Eve smiled, warmed by his certainty that they would remain in touch once she was gone, and a little saddened by the knowledge that under normal circumstances she was always too busy for friends.

"So, where did you learn to cook?" She asked, changing the subject.

"I've lived alone for a long time," he replied. "Long, lonely evenings are always made better by a nice meal."

"Funny, I always thought the opposite. I've eaten alone in so many restaurants that it always just makes me feel even lonelier." Eve couldn't remember the last proper dinner she had sat down to without having a book to hand to ensure she had something to do between courses.

"So what, you live to work *and* you eat to live?" He raised a brow. "That sounds like no fun at all. I've always been very much a live to eat guy."

"Your friends must love coming over here, I certainly would if I had friends who cooked like you."

A strange look flashed across Matthew's face.

"I don't have all that many friends."

"That surprises me. Why's that?"

A flash of something Eve couldn't decipher flickered across his face.

"Not really my sort around here," he said eventually. "They're all either stuck up housewives or just plain anti-social." On seeing Eve's frown, he smiled again. "And you, what's your social life like?"

"Sparse." Eve laughed.

"What about family?"

"Family?" Eve raised a brow. "Trust me, if we start talking about my family we'd be here all night. I got out of that a long time ago."

"You make it sound like you're from a cult."

"You could say that." She rolled her eyes. "We do stay in touch via postcards and suchlike, it's more just that we're very different people. They have their life and I have mine. Oh, and of course there's David, but he's –"

"Your boyfriend?"

"My assistant." She corrected. "And I guess the closest thing to a friend I have."

Matthew appeared to relax a little as he raised his glass and clinked it against hers.

"Well, here's to new friends."

~

The strange feeling in Eve's gut had returned, the dull tugging sensation that told her that she wasn't where she was supposed to be. Even her feet felt restless as she padded around the house during the day. The message on the television screen hadn't changed in weeks and everything else was just rumour. She could feel it in the air that something was very wrong, just as she had back at the airport. The air crackled around her, still uncomfortably warm and filled with that same strange static that held the threat of a thunderstorm that never came. Sometimes, when she peered out the window at the glaring sun, she thought she could see a seam in the sky where it had come apart. It was as though the world was unravelling but she couldn't explain why. When she tried to tell Matthew one evening over dinner, he had laughed.

"You're cracking up, Evie."

Evie. It was the little pet name Matthew had taken it upon himself to give her, Eve didn't particularly like it, but she knew he was just being affectionate, so she let it slide. Despite her restlessness, there was something nice about having a friend like Matthew, one who cooked for her and played board games at night. They didn't have very much in common, but it was the first time she had paused to appreciate the company of others. That evening when they played drafts, Matthew won, but it was only because Eve got the feeling he would be a sore loser.

~

One morning, Eve walked out into the garden. The flowers had started to bloom and the grass had the pleasant shimmer of the sun reflecting off fresh summery dew. She breathed in the garden scent, doing her best to ignore the heavy static in the air. Matthew stood by the bird feeder filling it with seed, oblivious to her presence and Eve watched him fondly as she sipped her coffee.

A gentle thudding caught both their attention as a jogger came down the pavement in their direction. Her bright, strawberry blonde ponytail swished behind her as she appeared to radiate a sunshine all of her own. Eve watched her in awe, realising that she hadn't seen anyone other than Matthew and the delivery driver in several weeks. She smiled and waved at the woman, envious of her body which was somehow both slim and curvy at the same time, and a face that seemed to smile even though her lips weren't moving. Eve glanced down at her own body, swamped by one of Matthew's t-shirts and his jogging pants on which she'd had to pull the drawstring as tightly as possible so that they would stay up on her hips. There had been a gym at her office which she went to when she needed to clear her head, which was often. As a result, her body had always been lean and muscular, but never pleasantly curvy in the way the jogger was.

"You've got a cracking set on you, Jeanie!" Matthew called unexpectedly at the jogger who paused in confusion. She cocked her head quizzically to the side before looking momentarily horrified and shuffling away in embarrassment, ceasing jogging for fear of the movement it might cause. Matthew smirked unpleasantly. As he turned around, he looked surprised to see Eve looking at him in shock. His smirk vanished.

"It was just a joke," he mumbled.

~

That evening, Eve excused herself from dinner and instead took a sandwich to her room with her, where she read a book. Later that night, as she walked down the corridor to get herself a glass of water, she passed Matthew who said nothing, but gave her a look that prevented her from sleeping that night.

~

Late one afternoon, the tugging in Eve's stomach directed her out the front door. Despite being barefoot, she began to jog, relieved to find that she could still run with ease. Her feet padded silently on the tarmac pavement and dusty driveways. She wanted more than anything to be back in her office where she was comfortable, filled with purpose as she strived to make everything within her power bigger, better and richer. She missed having David by her side, diligently following her instructions and ensuring her life ran as smoothly as possible. When she thought of David, she felt a pang, not in a romantic sense but in a way that made her realise that in the years they had worked together he had been the closest thing to a best friend she had ever known. He had the kind of eyes that made Eve soften, large and chestnut brown with long dark lashes that caused him to appear slightly feminine. He would never have been described as a handsome man, but there was something inexplicably gentle and pleasing about his appearance.

Eve reached the edge of the forest where the line of trees closed in tightly to create a distinct divide between land that belonged to the hamlet and the land that belonged to the forest. The spindly branches reached out as though they wanted to brush against Eve's face, she recoiled instinctively despite the pull that wanted her to go into woods.

"Eve! What the hell are you doing?"

Whipping around, Eve saw Matthew running towards her. Without her heels, she was several inches shorter than him. He perspired within his thick sheepskin coat, a strange choice for such a hot day.

"I was jogging," Eve replied stiffly.

"Everyone's supposed to stay inside, you know that."

"Then what are you doing outside?"

"I was worried about you."

"I needed to get out."

"Is my company really *that* bad?"

"I didn't say that." As Eve opened her mouth to state that she planned on staying out a little longer, she was already being steered back in the direction of the house. Her natural response would have been to smack Matthew's hand away, but something inside warned her not to and instead she followed him compliantly back to the house. When Matthew went to the kitchen to get dinner on the stove, Eve tried to find her car keys in her handbag, but they were nowhere to be found.

~

"Evie, wake up."

Eve awoke, disorientated in the darkness. She fumbled her hand around the cord of the lamp on the bedside table before turning it on and squinting. Matthew was perched quietly on the edge of her bed.

"*What the hell.*" She tugged the duvet up so that it covered her exposed shoulders, clutching it tightly.

"I'm sorry." Matthew held up his hands in a gesture that was supposed to convey that he meant no harm. "I just wanted to talk to you. Things have felt a little tense between us over the past few days. I wanted to clear the air."

"Okay, well consider the air cleared." Eve snapped. "Now can you leave me to get back to sleep, please?"

"Evie, you're being rude and I don't know why." Matthew looked at her with a lopsided smile. "There's been this tension and I think I know why."

"Oh?"

"I'll say it first if I have to – I love you, Evie, and I think you feel the same way about me." Planting his hand firmly on top of Eve's, she noticed it was unnaturally hot and clammy, which was little wonder given he was still wearing his thick coat. "You have such beautiful blue eyes, you know that?"

"No, stop it." Pulling her hand away, she shook her head. For a moment, Eve could have sworn that she saw Matthew's eyes flash red, like a dog's eyes would reflect light in the darkness. It was little more than a flicker against the glimmer of the lamp before they were back to normal again, an unremarkable grey green. He stared at her in silence for several seconds longer than was comfortable.

"You know something," his voice lowered into something that resembled a growl. "You're a bitch. *A total fucking bitch*. You swan in here and take advantage of my hospitality, let me make you breakfast, pour your coffee, cook your meals – you even called it a date!" His expression darkened. "You're as bad as the rest of those stuck-up bitches around here – I can't trust any of you. You know, I saw it – I saw the look in your eye when I cooked you that first meal, like you were surprised that a guy like me could actually cook – but you just think you're better than everyone else with your important job and your fancy suits. I bet you were the same when you were working, taking advantage of everyone around you – *absorbing them*. Well to hell with you, Eve." He rose to his feet, shuddering with rage as he leaned forward. "Just look around you, you have nothing other than my generosity and I tell you," Eve could feel his hot breath, "it's wearing *very* fucking thin."

Realising that she had been holding her breath, Eve exhaled, ensuring not to let herself tremble as she forced a small smile.

"Matthew," she said softly, "I'm so sorry. You're right. I've been so ungrateful. Why don't we have dinner tomorrow and we can talk about everything properly, maybe when I'm not so tired?"

Matthew's face softened and he blinked as though coming out of a trance.

"Yeah, of course." He smiled, nodding. "That would be great. I have seafood in the freezer, I could make that spaghetti you like?"

"That would be perfect."

"All right." He patted her arm with a hand that had ceased to be clammy. "You get some sleep."

As Matthew turned to leave the room, Eve's hand crept to the drawer by the bedside table and as though sensing what she was about to do, Matthew paused and turned his head, casting her a chilling smile.

"By the way, if you're looking for your phone, I noticed it was broken so I threw it out."

~

A few hours after Matthew had gone to bed that night, Eve crept out of her room, reassured by the soft snores coming from his bedroom, a noise she had become accustomed to over the weeks. With her bag slung over her shoulder, she tiptoed towards the front door and carefully turned the handle. It had been locked and the key was gone. Refusing to allow herself to panic, Eve moved towards the windows and tried to slide them open until she noticed that they had also been locked. Retreating into the living room, she crept over to an old desk in the hope of finding the keys in one of the drawers. As she fumbled in the darkness, her hands found several cables creeping from the wall and into the desk, when she pulled open the drawer, she was relieved to find a landline telephone inside. She couldn't remember the last time she had used one of those.

Carefully picking up the receiver, she punched in 999. However, to her dismay she was greeted with one long, abandoning beep. Swearing again, she searched her memory for any other number. When she was young, she could recall all her friend's landline telephone numbers but now, with mobile phones, she couldn't remember any of them. Except one. Her fingers carefully explored the buttons as she repeated the number softly under her breath, she could only really remember it if she repeated it in a singsong way. Her heart leapt as it began to ring.

"Hello?"

"*David!* Oh, thank God, David."

"Eve! Are you all right? I tried calling you after our last conversation, but the phones were down for a while and then I couldn't get through at all!"

"I'm not all right, David. You need to listen to me very carefully, I'm in trouble, and —"

Eve paused, realising she could no longer hear the steady, relaxed snores of Matthew and instead it had turned into shallow breathing that sounded closer than his bedroom. Turning to the door, she saw that Matthew filled the frame, his eyes glimmering a furious red in the darkness. Eve began to scream, a horrible, terrorised noise that she didn't know she was capable of making.

"*David, help me*!"

The phone was whipped from her hand as cords were ripped from the wall and the device shattered beneath Matthew's foot on the floor beside her. Suddenly she was on her side, a heavy impact against her forehead causing an explosion of pain behind her eyes. Dazed, she felt her body being dragged slowly across the carpet.

"Here." A gentle voice whispered in her ear. Grey green eyes blinked next to hers. "Take this for the pain."

~

Eve awoke on the sofa, a throbbing pressure pulsating through her ears and pressing against the back of her eyeballs. Her voice croaked as she tried to speak.

"Shh." A damp cloth pressed against her forehead and retracted; white cotton stained with angry crimson. "It's a good thing I'm a first aider; that was a nasty knock you took."

"Please, Matthew." The room was dimly lit by a nearby lamp and each time the light caught Matthew's eyes, they glimmered red.

"Shh," he repeated, turning away from the light so that his eyes returned to green.

Feeling the tugging in her stomach again, more intensely than ever, Eve let it pull her up into a sitting position, her spine suddenly rigid. As if guided like a puppet, her arms thrust out with a strength that was new to her and caught Matthew in the centre of his chest. He tumbled back with a surprised roar. The pulling sensation hauled Eve to her feet and guided her down the corridor, urging her to ignore the pain in her skull. As she reached the door, the narrow panes shattered spontaneously and somehow her body slid through the gap that couldn't have been more than several inches in width. The pulling manoeuvred her body into a skilful roll so that she was back on her feet and standing barefoot beneath the light of the silvery moon. Glancing behind her, she saw Matthew's arm still trying to grapple for her through the gap. His arm caught against a shard of glass, drawing a crimson line across his elbow. Red eyed, he stared at it before dipping his finger in the blood and running it across the intact pane, his finger formed the words CAN'T TRUST ANY OF THEM.

Eve whipped around. As her feet pounded down the pavement to the end of the hamlet, she plunged into the dense forest, submerged in shadow and refusing to stop as the spindly branches slashed against her cheeks and eyes. The pull in her stomach had taken over her movements and was only getting stronger. Instinctively, she knew she was close.

As she reached a clearing in the middle of the forest, the pulling stopped and gave one sharp tug down towards the ground before vanishing completely. Eve pressed her hands against her stomach, quietly begging the feeling to come back and continue to guide her to safety. Without it, she felt alone and afraid.

Glancing down at the soft earth, her toes began to wriggle and disappear into the soil. Something told her that going down was her only way out, so she began to move her entire body in a strange and unfamiliar motion, like a corkscrew, that allowed her to descend deeper into the ground. As the dirt reached her knees, Matthew burst into the clearing, his eyes ablaze and fingers curled, claw-like. He was sniffing like an animal hunting prey, testing the air until his furious gaze settled on Eve who was firmly rooted in place.

"Matthew, please!" She screamed. "You're my friend! Please don't hurt me!"

Tears sprang from Eve's eyes, streaming down her face and between trembling lips.

"I just wanted you to love me." His voice was barely audible beneath the unnatural growl. "All I ever wanted was for someone to love me."

Crouching on his haunches, Matthew readied himself to leap onto Eve, claws ready and strings of saliva stretching between his teeth. As he did so, another figure appeared from the darkness of the trees. A little girl. She was dressed in what looked like a costume from a bad school play, a thick grey cloak over a green onesie and a jewelled crown atop her head of ginger curls.

"*No!*" Eve waved furiously at the child. "Run away! Go and get help!"

Instead of looking frightened, the girl's lips curled into a smile, and she made a gentle calming gesture in Eve's direction. Matthew turned to face her, his anger at the interruption burning across his face. As he readied himself to swipe the little girl aside, her smile vanished and she opened her mouth impossibly wide, revealing a set of monstrous, jagged teeth. Before Matthew could react she was upon him, pinning him to the ground and burying her face into his neck as he writhed beneath her small body. Several long minutes passed and Matthew's struggling became slower and weaker. Before he had stopped moving completely, the little girl pulled herself from him and wiped her mouth with her sleeve.

"A princess is merciful," she said eventually. Rising to her feet, she picked up the wooden staff that she had been carrying before the attack and pointed it at Matthew's limp body. "Everyone deserves to be loved," she murmured. "But not everyone deserves to be loved in the way they want to be."

Matthew's body began to writhe and distort beneath the wooden staff. Eve covered her eyes in horror as his bones cracked hideously and hair sprouted from his body. Seconds later, a large dog lay whimpering on the ground.

"Perhaps someone will love you now." The girl prodded the dog with her stick until it dragged itself away into the forest. Casting Eve a brief smile, the girl waved cheerily and vanished in the opposite direction.

"Eve!" As if on cue, another figure staggered through the trees, breathless and clothes damp with sweat. David appeared before her, large brown eyes wide in confusion as he looked her up and down.

"Oh, David!" Eve cried, struggling in the dirt. "How did you find me?"

"I got the area code and your solicitor to give me the address," he hesitated. "You signed a mandate a while back so I could deal with your legal stuff, remember?" Pausing, he looked around at the empty clearing. "I heard you screaming. What the hell's going on?"

Eve began to cry; loud gasping sobs made her body shudder in the ground.

"It's okay – I'm here!" David rushed to her side, wrapping his arms around her and trying to ease her gently from the earth that had half consumed her. She collapsed into his familiar peppermint chewing gum scent, relishing the feel of his warm hands pressed against her back.

Suddenly, the pulling sensation returned in her stomach. Filled with exhaustion, Eve felt her willpower vanish and her body begin to drag slowly downwards.

"I've got you." David gripped her tighter. "I hope you know, Eve, I would do *anything* for you." As his breath brushed her face, Eve felt the tugging take control of her body again and begin burrowing furiously downwards, as though something was growing beneath her, like plant roots in the ground. David's eyes widened as Eve watched him begin to burrow down alongside her. The static air crackled around them and their hearts pumped in perfect unison as they began to turn in a corkscrew motion together.

"What's happening?" David's voice was shrill as he continued to hold onto Eve, refusing to let go. His cries became gradually quieter and Eve realised that it was her who was crying out in David's voice. The roots that grew from her legs were dragging David down and consuming him. His beautiful brown eyes had developed an unpleasant milky sheen and his cheeks were growing hollow. Eve began to scream, an amalgamation of her voice and David's.

"No!" She screamed, trying to grasp at David's lifeless body. "No, *David*!"

"I love you, Eve." The male voice came from Eve's lips, one final gasp before she swallowed his voice and David was consumed entirely by her roots that wriggled through the earth. As though filled with a fresh energy, the roots began to grow at a more rapid pace, winding and pushing through the dirt, guided by the pulling sensation. Taking control of Eve's body, they pulled her down into the earth like a plant receding for winter and she began to follow them down into the darkness. Fuelled by David who enabled her to dig deeper, her hand plunged out into a great cavernous space below her. As the earth that created the ceiling began to crumble, she screamed at the prospect of the drop into what appeared to be a vast stone tunnel. However, before she fell, her roots wrapped around her waist, acting like a harness and pressed into her back like warm hands as David's strength eased her gently to a wooden table surface down below. The roots recoiled from the ceiling, creeping slowly back inside Eve's body.

Eve looked around her as she lay on the table in amongst glasses, bottles and decks of cards. The air around her was a fug of smoke as a group of elderly women sat in armchairs and stared at her, not looking as surprised as they ought to have been. A cluster of aunts, old cousins and her grandmother.

"*Eve*?" Her aunt raised a sparse eyebrow. "We haven't seen you in a long time – not even a postcard this year. I take it you've come to escape the end of the world too?"

SIX

The Dollhouse Gallery

Robyn

Every version of this note is slightly different, although I do try to replicate them as best I can to ensure that there is context to my work. It's very hard to say how long I've been here, in this place where day and night doesn't exist. Clocks don't function in this house, and I don't feel the urge to sleep any more. Time slithers by unnoticed.

I am completely lost in this house, and lately I'm starting to realise that, on a balance of probabilities, I'm never getting out. I don't know how to feel about that, since I don't think it's possible for people to truly understand or visualise eternity. The irony is that, even if I wanted to escape, the longer I'm here the deeper I need to go into the house just to survive. It's a bit like the fridge: the fridge is always fully stocked with food, but once I've eaten everything, I need to go inside the next house to find the next fridge. I appreciate that it probably sounds like I'm rambling, but please don't dismiss me yet, read my story first and maybe then you will understand the work I'm doing here. The deeper you go to read me, the closer you might come to finding me.

~

My name is Robyn Hendrie. An ex-boyfriend once described me as a 'self-proclaimed artist' which was quite frankly insulting because I did actually go to art school, a good one at that. Coming from a family of accountants and shop managers, my decision had been heavily frowned upon. '*You'll never make a comfortable living drawing pictures, Robyn*' my mother once uttered tersely at a family event. The low hum of surrounding accountants (they do make that collective sound; I don't think I'm just imagining it?) rose an octave in agreement. Infuriatingly, they had turned out to be right. As my friends became increasingly well-known and widely exhibited, my work stagnated. Jealousy poisoned my art as I desperately tried to emulate their work and successes, resulting in something profoundly uninspired. The most frustrating part of it was that I used to be good; I used to be *really* good.

Eventually, I admitted defeat and moved back up north where my family were from. Living in the city had become too expensive and by that point I was too old to rely on the allure of being a struggling artist to justify my lifestyle and unpaid rent. I had started to look tired; the stress of my financial burdens began carving lines into my once smooth complexion. My mother said to me *'there's a point, Robyn, where a woman needs to start making a bit more effort'*. I screamed internally when she said that, but I didn't respond. My aunt did my parents a favour by hiring me at her accountancy firm in town in a well-paid administrative role where they gave me fair holidays and a little Christmas bonus. At intervals between Monday and Friday, 9am to 5pm, I hovered near the small clusters of suits, skirts and ties that gathered around the coffee machine and listened as they enthusiastically discussed reality television and gym classes. At first, I spent the day trying to swallow the unpleasant lump in my throat that was made up with a paradoxical mix of envy and contempt; but then I signed up for the gym classes and turned on the television. Eventually I merged with the cluster of suits, skirts and ties and found myself in the conflicted position of enjoying the company and routine, and despising the direction my life had taken.

At the weekends, I rented a stall at the Saturday craft fair, nestled in amongst scented beeswax candles, misshapen silver jewellery and an alpaca knits stall run by a clique of old ladies who I suspected of pouring sherry into their thermos flasks. I would buy a hot chocolate from one of the stalls and sip it leisurely throughout the day, and once it was time to close up I would go home and run a bath for 7pm, lighting one of my beeswax candles and disappearing into a lavender soak. It all seemed very decadent at first, but then it became an unavoidable Saturday habit that caused me inexplicable stress if it wasn't strictly adhered to. Bath at 7pm, television until 10:30pm and in bed by 11pm. One Saturday, the craft fair was closed because of the weather, and I found myself unable to settle until Monday when my weekly routine reset.

I didn't set out to make dollhouses, it came about when I decided to make a miniature living room display for my stall with tiny versions of my paintings so that people might see what they would look like framed on their walls. I cut out little carpets and even filed down tiny skirting boards to mimic the appearance of a living room. People were fascinated by the details in the rooms, and they would come by my stall simply to coo at the displays. Because I didn't need the money from my art, the attention became my primary form of currency at the fair and I made more and more miniature displays, forgoing my paintings for the satisfaction of creating perfect little spaces. When I heard news of one of my old friend's exhibition successes, where there would once have been an unpleasant knot of envy and regret at the direction of my own art career, I simply sat at my desk with my materials and forgot about my discontent as I measured, carved, sanded, painted and polished. My pointless little pieces of furniture were a thing of precise beauty: a petrol blue velvet chaise-longue that sat against an elaborate bay window beneath an ornate ceiling rose; even the grey carpeted display of generic cream furniture that mimicked my own suburban hell.

The arts and crafts fair was where I met a woman called Helen McIvor. That's how all this started, back before things got strange. I recognised her as she approached my stall because she was there most Saturday's. She struck me as the kind of woman who would profess to buy everything local while dolled up in the latest designer gear. Her glow was less radiant and more waxwork, but at least she kept her smile politely in place. Leaning over my stall, she took particular interest in a little novelty display I had constructed. It was a living room with tiny, handmade pieces of furniture and miniature copies of my paintings in little frames hanging from the walls.

"That's *adorable*!" She gushed, stroking the velvet on the model armchair. "I have a chair *exactly* like this!"

I smiled politely back.

"Can you make dollhouses?" She asked, raising an immaculately plucked brow. "You see, it's my daughter's birthday and I'm wanting to give her something special."

"I only make room displays. I've never made an actual house before."

"I asked *can* you, not have you." Her tone caught me off guard, and before I knew it, I had agreed to make her daughter a dollhouse.

Helen's request was unusual, she wanted an exact replica of her own house made, right down to the furniture and appliances. *Right down to the plug sockets in the walls*, she said. I suspect I would have agreed, even without the ludicrous sum that she was offering to pay me for it. The thought of a project so precise and detailed sent a strange jolt of satisfaction through me. If anything, it was something to throw myself at and forget the disappointments of my creative career to date.

When I went over to her place to take measurements, I met her two glossy haired daughters with their fixed smiles who greeted me politely at the entrance to their airy, pastel blue hallway. Her husband Paul looked at her in a way that, despite him saying nothing the entire time I was there, suggested he couldn't stand her. Everything about her home made me uncomfortable. My boots suddenly felt dirty and clunky in the presence of immaculate heels and white tennis shoes as I navigated her pristine lawn. The house itself was a perfectly co-ordinated display of pastels and untouched furniture. I felt awkward and clumsy even when I was standing still.

Anyway, I digress. So shortly after this, things got strange and we all had to stay at home. My aunt shut down the accountancy firm and I didn't have a job to go to; so instead, I threw myself into Helen's dollhouse. I watched YouTube videos to help me with the structure and I ordered all sorts of beautiful fabrics and materials from the internet to make the furniture just right. By that time, I also had a boyfriend: Martin. We went on our first date shortly before things became strange and by virtue of that, we became close more quickly than we would have done under normal circumstances. We weren't right for each other, but during that time it didn't really matter.

Martin was a delivery driver for a local butcher and after things got strange, demand for them skyrocketed. When Martin's supervisor Billy went missing, he took over all the rural deliveries and he was compensated well for it.

The dollhouse kept me sane through those strange first few weeks.

I had planned on waiting until it was all over to take the dollhouse to Helen, however, I knew that her daughter's birthday was coming up later that week and I imagined it was a tough time for kids. Since Martin did deliveries in that area anyway, I asked him if I could join him to drop it off. Technically he should have refused, but Martin never could say no to me. Besides, his new van was kitted out with all those fancy new alarms and unbreakable glass, the recommended model for delivery drivers since things got strange. There had been horror stories about delivery drivers hauled from their vehicles by folk who had lost their grip on reality and dragged into the trees or away into the hills, never to be seen or heard from again. That was what they reckoned had happened to Billy, since he had gone out in one of the old vans. The vehicle had been found empty and unlocked in a passing place in the middle of nowhere. Martin's boss had found it, but he didn't bother recovering it. It still sat there at the side of the road just outside of town. We said nothing as we passed it.

Martin parked up outside Helen's front gate in the picturesque little hamlet wedged between sea and forest. My eyes widened at her previously immaculate garden which was now piled with televisions and various boxes, some of which had toppled and crushed her lovely flower patches. Martin asked me to check with her if it was for the skip because if so, we'd happily take some of it home. Carefully, I removed the dollhouse from the back of the van, wedged between packaged meat and egg boxes and walked up her path to the front door. My eyes flickered warily from side to side. The door was open. I called out and tried her mobile, but nobody answered, so I went inside.

Other than a shattered mirror in one of the bathrooms, everything seemed to be in place, just as it had been the last time I had been at the house. Setting up the dollhouse on the side table in the blue hallway, I opened its front and removed the miniature televisions and appliances and broke the little mirror, spreading its shards across the replica bathroom so that the two houses would be identical in every way. Taking a step back, I paused to consider my work.

Something was wrong with the dollhouse.

That was when I realised what the problem was, and I kicked myself for not noticing it sooner. There was no dollhouse in the dollhouse. If it was going to be just right, then there would have to be a replica dollhouse in the dollhouse on the living room coffee table. Fortunately, I had my tools in the van just in case I noticed something like that, so I went and removed them, asking Martin if he could finish his deliveries and come pick me up when he was done. He queried whether it was right for me to be in someone's house without their permission, but I lied and said I had texted Helen to let her know.

Getting to work on the tiny house within the dollhouse, I took painstaking care to make it an exact replica of the dollhouse I had just made. Of course, once it was complete, another dollhouse needed to be made within that dollhouse. The more I thought about it, the more the project seemed like the kind of quirky thing a gallery owner would love. My eyes ached through the magnifying glass as I squinted at the miniscule features, and my tools became smaller and more intricate, causing my hands to ache from the exertion of being so delicate.

Once I got into the swing of it, the tiny houses and the interiors became much easier to make, and I hardly needed to use any materials. Everything came together with ease. I couldn't be certain how long I spent making the little houses, or how many I had actually made by that point, but when I finally blinked and checked the clock on the hallway wall, I noticed that the second hand was motionless and assumed it was broken. However, it was bright outside, if a little dull, so I assumed it must have been early evening. Checking my phone, I realised that the battery had died, which probably meant Martin had been waiting for me for some time outside. Straightening the dollhouse on the table, I wiped the perspiration from my brow and stretched my spine until it made a satisfying crunch. As I opened the front door and stepped out, I realised that instead of being in the garden where it ought to have led me, I had walked back into the hallway that I had left. I furrowed my brow, assuming that exhaustion was meddling with my cognition and returned to the front door to try again. I walked out the front door and back into the hallway. After three more attempts, I began to panic and call for help, racing up and down the floors of the house calling Martin's name.

Clambering up into Helen's loft, I piled several immaculately labelled storage boxes on top of one another to allow me to climb up and peer out of the sloping roof window. Pulling myself up on the tips of my fingers, the scene that greeted me was no longer a garden leading out onto a quiet road, but a colossal staircase and a span of pastel blue that you could be forgiven for confusing with a gloomy sky at first glance. I realised that the light I thought I had seen shining through the windows was simply from the lamp that was turned on beside the dollhouse on the hallway table.

~

I'm no great writer, so I find it hard to put in words the horror that I felt in that moment. After running through countless dollhouses, I crumpled in a heap and sobbed into the oatmeal rug which smelt like a strange mixture of glue and varnish. I couldn't say how long I spent lying there; as I said, time slithers by here. It could be months or even years that I've been here now. I've taken to making myself gourmet meals every night using Helen's handwritten recipe book, a copy of which I find in each version of the house that I travel through. My favourite recipe is the duck egg and asparagus salad, but unfortunately Helen only stocked the fridge with chicken eggs, so I suppose I'll never be able to make it properly, which is a pity.

Once the fear subsided and I resigned myself to a life in the dollhouses, boredom began to set in. I became restless, working my way through Helen's shelves of books, which were all smutty holiday reads and self-help guides. Fortunately, whilst exploring the loft, I opened up her storage boxes to find some art supplies in amongst old pantomime props. Helen's walls became my canvas. My enthusiasm for painting was rejuvenated as I played with colour and form, creating a series of intricate studies of the flowers in vases as they gradually wilted and died throughout the course of my stay in each house. They varied from fine illustrations to great, abstract pieces that spread across her ceiling and marble countertops.

~

Now I spend each day in front of the walls, and each house I move through; I create something new and entirely different; a fresh study of whatever I find that piques my interest. I have found fascination in the mundane. Sometimes the houses are beautiful, sometimes haunting and other times they are entirely grotesque, but each house is wonderful in its own way.

~

This little exhibition note is now complete and the fridge in this house is empty, but I will be sure to write a copy of my story in each house that I move through in the hope that someday someone will find it and understand my work. One day, the art world will talk about the woman from the dollhouse, so that either way, whether it's here or there, I will live forever.

Welcome to The Dollhouse Gallery.

SEVEN

JEANIE

Jeanie

Nobody had ever told Jeanie that her life would be as good as it turned out to be, although everyone had always known that she would do well, since Jeanie had an enviable habit of always being in the right place at the right time.

When Jeanie got her first job, she was at a careers fair and had accidentally bumped into the company CEO. The CEO liked her immediately and offered her the position there and then; after all, Jeanie was undeniably charming.

The man who later became her husband had ended up on the same chairlift as her when she was out skiing one weekend. She had been disgruntled because her three friends from work, with whom she had gone skiing, had taken the other lift to her exclusion rather than doing two and two which Jeanie had thought would be far fairer. However, it had worked out for the best, and she didn't speak to those friends any more.

Jeanie's husband later became an overnight success following a savvy investment after a chance encounter with a couple 'in the know'. They met in a cooking class that Jeanie arranged for her husband's birthday. Jeanie and her husband went on to buy the kind of home they could only ever have dreamed of; a beautiful old farmhouse that had been left derelict for years. It sat on a hill overlooking a quaint little hamlet that sat between sea and forest. It was the kind of place that had warped with age, with creaky floorboards and cracked walls. Jeanie loved the character and imperfection of it all. She began fixing it up as soon as they moved in, making it a real home for her and her husband. Jeanie had stopped working by that point, since her husband had told her that there was no need for her to do anything that she didn't enjoy any more. '*Isn't he sweet?*' They would say, '*isn't he just perfectly sweet?*'

Her husband had surprised her by creating a beautiful music room, the kind of space that house guests couldn't help but enviably compliment when they were over. Bright white, with high ceilings, bold velvet furniture and Jeanie's cello in pride of place since music was her passion. Or so she thought.

After the warning to stay home, Jeanie found that her life didn't actually change all that much. Her husband's line of work remained essential, so he still went to work every day and Jeanie would sit at home and wait for him as she had done every day since they had moved in. Very few of her friends had visited her new home. Like many others, Jeanie found that as she got older, her friendship group became smaller and less substantial. Some moved away as Jeanie had done, others had children; there were divorces, separations and the rest simply drifted apart. As Jeanie's mother had bluntly put it *'that's just life'*.

As Jeanie sat alone in the music room, she paused to assess her passion for music. Music was one of those things that people advised parents to get their children into because, for whatever reason, it made them more successful later in life. Jeanie had gone to weekly cello lessons as a child, during which an old woman in a smelly cardigan would bark and make her start over and over and over. Jeanie hadn't enjoyed it one bit. What Jeanie had enjoyed about music was when guests were over for dinner parties and she could end the night by playing them something beautiful that they would remember.

However, Jeanie hadn't thrown a dinner party in some time. Even before things got strange, her neighbours in the hamlet hadn't seemed like her kind of people, and being in the wrong company was always the loneliest place to be. So instead, Jeanie sat alone in her music room, holding her bow in one hand but not making a sound. She hadn't made a sound in a long time.

One morning, Jeanie's husband leaned in to kiss her goodbye. He always left early for work and came back late, a consequence of them moving so far out into the countryside. Jeanie never worried about him, because nothing bad ever happened in her life so she knew he would be absolutely fine, despite the dangers that lurked outside their front door. She let him kiss her and made up a story about how she was learning a new Bach piece. Her husband told her that he couldn't wait to hear it, although they both knew that it would be so late by the time he got home that they would both forget and go to bed, which was a blessing, since Jeanie hadn't actually learnt a new piece in a long time.

Sometimes Jeanie wanted him to catch her out, to find out that she was taking advantage of his kind offer to allow her to pursue her passions. *'Isn't he sweet'* she remembered how they used to chant it like a mantra, *'encouraging your passion'*.

'I'm not passionate', she wanted to scream.

Her husband stepped out the door that same morning, getting into his car and rumbling down their immaculate gravel drive, vanishing through the groomed archway of foliage and shrubbery by the gate. In the distance, the sea sparkled in a great glittering expanse and the mountains in the distance were losing their snowy peaks as summer crept up their frozen summits. Taking a deep breath, Jeanie wondered what she was going to do with her day. She wasn't supposed to leave the house, but as she knew, nothing bad ever happened to her.

Slipping on her lycra running gear, she pulled her long, strawberry blonde hair into a high ponytail and jogged down into the hamlet with a resolution that she would try and make friends with her neighbours; even if they couldn't have dinner parties for the time being, it would be nice to say hello to someone new. As she descended into the cluster of houses, she glanced back up at her looming home on the hill and realised that she must look like a queen in her castle overlooking a small kingdom.

Up ahead, behind a white fence, a man wearing a sheepskin coat stood by a bird feeder. Several feet from him, a dark-haired woman stared at her for a moment before a smile formed on her lips. Jeanie opened her mouth to say something friendly but was abruptly interrupted.

"You've got a cracking set on you, Jeanie!" The man shouted, casting her an unpleasant and leering look. Shocked, Jeanie stopped, waiting for the woman who she presumed was his wife to say something. The woman stayed quiet. Cheeks burning, Jeanie walked swiftly away and took the next turn back up the hill to her street, to avoid passing that house again.

When she returned home her heart was still pounding from embarrassment and anger. She had no plans to go out jogging again.

Returning to her music room and leaning her cello between her thighs, Jeanie considered how all she seemed to do these days was wait for her husband to come home. It occurred to her that she was wasting her life waiting instead of enjoying what she had to offer. If she couldn't be happy in her own company, how could she expect to be happy in the company of others?

Laying down her cello, she strolled to the front door where her hand touched the smooth wood and slid up to the metal bolt. She pushed the door slowly shut and bolted it from the inside. A tiny, uncertain laugh formed in her throat as she wondered what would happen if she left the door bolted; it was old and thick, impossible to break down. Wandering back to her music room, she sat quietly for the remainder of the day.

That evening, there was a knock on the door. It was her husband. His keys wouldn't work because the door was bolted from the inside and he was calling out for her to let him in. Jeanie turned the lights out and sat in the kitchen, waiting until he left. Once he was gone, she reheated some soup from the fridge and ate her dinner in silence. Jeanie felt a strange and inexplicable surge of excitement in the pit of her stomach. She didn't have to wait for anyone any more.

The banging against the windows went on for a number of days, perhaps even weeks. Jeanie felt a bit bad because her husband had obviously taken time off work to try and reason with her. He was far too busy for that, particularly with everything that had been going on.

Later, Jeanie's in-laws turned up and started banging on the door too. At first, they were kind, asking her what the matter was. They said that strange things had been happening and they wondered if something strange was happening to Jeanie too. Then, when she didn't answer, they got angry. They shouted at her and called her ungrateful and cruel, they told her how upset her husband was.

All the while, Jeanie felt a strange thrill bubbling inside her. Her sister-in-law threatened to break a window but when Jeanie stood in front of the glass, not looking at anything in particular, her sister-in-law backed away, dropping the rock from her hand. They left. Jeanie's parents arrived a few days after that, her husband had obviously gone to them for help. They were too frightened to stay for very long, but they slipped a note through the letterbox. Jeanie didn't read it. She left it on the porch tiles where the mice nibbled the edges for their nests. The mice left their droppings all over the tiles which had gone from being slick with polish to dull and dusty. It felt as though several years had passed, but that couldn't possibly be right.

Jeanie awoke one evening to a strange whining sound at the front door. Peering out the windows to ensure it wasn't an ambush, she unbolted it and peered out at the doorstep. A large, limping dog shivered in the darkness. For a moment, she considered shooing it away, but her conscience got the better of her and she patted its head, allowing it to stagger inside. She slammed the door and bolted it firmly behind the creature.

"Poor thing." She whispered, offering the weak creature some sausages which it devoured gratefully and nuzzled affectionately by her side.

Jeanie started to share her meals with the dog. Down in the basement, she found venison fillet steaks in the freezer which she brought up and let defrost on the kitchen counter. Once they had defrosted, Jeanie didn't bother to cook them, instead, she sat on the floor with the dog and bit into her share. A trickle of blood ran down her chin as she looked into the dog's wide grey green eyes. She grinned at the dog and the dog grinned back.

One day, Jeanie's skin fell off. It crumpled to the floor like an old dress.

~

You see, I haven't been entirely honest with you. Jeanie is not a real person and she never has been. She was just one of many skins that I wore to try and fit in. As it turned out, Jeanie was my favourite. It started off as a bit of fun and I tried her on now and again, fastening her up at the back so that she was snug against my body. She nipped in all my less elegant body parts, tight across my stomach and pleasantly padded at the rear. Her hair was long and lustrous, with skin so soft and smooth that I had to stop myself from stroking it in public. People looked at me and they loved me. Old friends were replaced with new ones who were only familiar with the Jeanie skin. Before too long, I realised that with Jeanie, all my wishes came true. The CEO of the company I had so desperately wanted to work for was so taken by her that she offered her the job on the spot. The man on the chairlift fell in love with her instantly and the couple at the culinary class couldn't wait to offer some sage advice to the wonderfully delightful Jeanie who deserved only the best out of life.

I didn't mean to wear Jeanie so often but after a time it just became easier. I noticed the little things at first, such as when I wore Jeanie out with my in-laws, they seemed to like me. When I didn't wear Jeanie, they glowered and excluded me from events. Jeanie became part of their family where I never would be. I started making a point to always wear Jeanie around them. I wore Jeanie on my wedding day and after we were married, when I didn't wear her, my husband said I looked tired. Even my own family seemed to prefer Jeanie's fixed smile to my wavering uncertainty. Jeanie played the cello beautifully and everyone loved her.

I left Jeanie on the floor in a crumpled heap. My body felt peculiar, lumpier than I recalled. I was bald and my skin had a strange slimy texture to it, like a newborn, sticky with amniotic fluid. The dog watched me uncertainly, slowly approaching and giving me a cursory sniff before satisfying itself that it was me. It licked me clean. I bent down on my hands and knees so that it could clean behind my ears, and then, turning to Jeanie's crumpled, lifeless heap on the floor, we approached her on all fours, tearing her to shreds with our teeth and claws. Once we were finished with her, we looked at each other. We were hungry. All the food in the house had been eaten some time ago.

I dragged myself down the corridor, stretching one spindly hand after the next as I adjusted to my new body. I passed the bathroom, crawling closer to the front door where the dog looked expectantly up at the bolt. I was surprised initially that there was no mail, but then I remembered that the postmen didn't work any more. Slipping my hand up to the bolt, I hesitated for just a moment, glancing at the dog who watched me quietly. It nodded encouragingly, looking at me with its large green eyes and telling me that it loved the creature inside the Jeanie skin. The door swung open and I held my breath.

I blinked, squinting at the pale yellow of the morning sun that hurt my eyes. The grass on our lawn was far longer than the last time I had seen it and the gravel was overgrown with moss, the unusual heat of that summer had accelerated the growth of everything green. I wondered how long it had been since my husband had given up on me and left for good. There were no fresh tracks in the gravel and the arch where our gate was overgrown and concealed by thick shrubs. Nobody had been here in a long time.

The dog and I stood side by side on the stone porch, letting our eyes which had grown used to the dark glimmer red against the sunlight. We tossed back our heads and we howled a beautiful, mournful song.

EIGHT
The Spaceman

They say that all stories are based on the truth in some way or another.

When the people from the other world eventually landed on the green planet, they wandered entranced through the overgrowth, and tentatively tested the air before removing their helmets, relishing the natural, breathable atmosphere that they had been in search of for a very long time. One shed a tear as he saw the vast seas sparkle before him. Seas and oceans had become obsolete back in their world.

Then they reached a cluster of houses in a tiny community between the sea and the woods. Similarly to the other places they had visited, the buildings were old and crumbling, and all the windows had been shattered. The forest had crept out and encroached on roads and paths, winding greenery through fence posts and creeping up brickwork. Given the infrastructure they had identified, they expected to see people that were somewhat like them living on the planet, but they found none, which led them to wonder what had happened to this vibrant world. They were unaware that it was their predecessors and their failed attempts to cross the dimensions of time and space that had terrorised this realm in centuries gone by. They did not realise that the seams of reality had been torn apart and the people that they were so eager to meet had suffered terribly. However, unlike their world, the green planet had succeeded in healing itself.

The visitors found handwritten stories and strange recordings that dated back hundreds of years, telling tales of places called 'hamlet' and 'clachan', stories of witches who had escaped the end of the world by retreating underground and living in sewers and tunnels, or the woman of the water who brought down the ships of men who tried to pollute her oceans. There was the monster that ran free in the hills with her red-eyed hound, they would lure in anyone who heard their beautiful song and condemn them to eternal infatuation. Then there was the story of the house with many doors, where lost souls would become trapped forever in their dreams.

The people from the other world ensured that each story they found was carefully stored in their archives so that their scholars could study the rich mythology of this place.

One of the men from the other world tucked his bubble helmet beneath his arm and loosened the fastenings on his green suit to cool himself against the stifling sunshine. He walked beyond the cluster of broken homes towards the thick forest, where he paused at the sight of movement. The foliage rustled ominously, and a small, white face appeared amongst the greenery. An orange-haired child in a tattered grey cloak with a glistening crown atop her head peered out at him with wild eyes. At first, she looked angry, pointing a wooden stick in his direction, then she squinted against the sunlight and dropped her weapon. Her eyes widened in astonishment.

The man from the other world raised his hands to indicate he meant no harm, and he watched as tears rolled from the little girls' eyes. She walked towards him, extending a small hand and stretching her mouth into a sharp toothed smile.

"It's me." Her breath was rapid with excitement as the man from the other world backed nervously away. "It's Polly."

About the Author

Joanna Corrance is a lawyer and author from the Highlands of Scotland. She writes dark speculative fiction, gothic horror and science fiction; her publications include the novella *John's Eyes* (Luna Press, 2021) and the horror novel *The Gingerbread Men* (Haunt Publishing, 2022).

ALSO FROM NEWCON PRESS

ANIMALS – Geoff Ryman

A powerful new novel from the multiple award-winning author of *HIM, Was* and *The Child Garden* The chilling tale of a family caught at the heart of a terrifying and transformative epidemic; an astonishing fusion of beautiful writing and pure horror as the world we know falls apart.

Rowany de Vere and a Fair Degree of Frost – Chaz Brenchley

Rowany has taken up service on Mars. As a spy. Her mission is to escort a prominent defector across the hostile surface of Mars, pursued by Russian agents. Success will require every ounce of her wits and her training, but, as it says on her card, she is Rowany de Vere. Of the Colonial Office.

The Creator – Aliya Whiteley

When Phillip receives a distraught call to say that his brother is dead, he doesn't hesitate in dashing to his sister-in-law's side. Little does he imagine the tragedy and horror that awaits ors what has really happened to the genius behind ThinkBulb, the invention that changed the world.

A Jura for Julia – Ken MacLeod

The first collection in eighteen years from multiple award-winning science fiction author Ken MacLeod. His finest previously published short stories and novelettes along with a new story written specially for this collection. Cover art and internal illustrations by **Fangorn**.